CRITICAL ACCLAIM FOR THE MYSTERIE OF CAROLYN WHEAT

Winner of the Anthony, Agatha, Macavity, and Shamus Awards

"Wheat's characterizations are lethal, and she doesn't let up... A strong, smart writer with a clear head for complicated matters and a kind eye for her characters' feelings."

—*New York Times Book Review*

"Dazzlingly plotted... Wheat is a natural storyteller."

—*Kirkus Reviews*

"Literate, witty... characters who have real depth and honest emotions."

—*Library Journal*

"An author who equals and even outstrips many established mystery writers in depth of plotting and intricate character development..."

—*Booklist*

"...promises all the tension and excitement of a great roller coaster ride. All you need to do is buckle your seat belt and hang on for dear life."

—*Mostly Murder*

"Carolyn Wheat...proves that she's the equal of any of the best writers."

—*Amazon.com Mystery Editor*

"Sharply drawn characters and incisively written scenes are the rule."

—*The Armchair Detective*

"Wheat spins a solid mystery... More impressively, she teases out many quirks of character..."

—*Publishers Weekly*

Also by Carolyn Wheat

THE CASS JAMESON SERIES
Dead Men's Thoughts
Where Nobody Dies
Fresh Kills
Mean Streak
Troubled Waters
Sworn To Defend

Tales Out of School (short fiction)

ANTHOLOGIES EDITED BY CAROLYN WHEAT
Murder on Route 66
Women Before the Bench

How To Write KiLLER Fiction

The Funhouse of Mystery
&
the Roller Coaster of Suspense

Carolyn Wheat

PALO ALTO :: SANTA BARBARA :: 2003
PERSEVERANCE PRESS :: JOHN DANIEL & COMPANY

For information concerning quantity discounts for educational institutions,
writing groups, conferences, etc., call 1-800-662-8351.

A Perseverance Press Book
Published by John Daniel & Company
A division of Daniel & Daniel, Publishers, Inc.
Post Office Box 21922
Santa Barbara, California 93121
www.danielpublishing.com/perseverance

10 9 8 7 6 5 4 3 2
10 09 08 07 06 05 04 03

Book design by Eric Larson, Studio E Books, Santa Barbara
www.studio-e-books.com

LIBRARY OF CONGRESS CATALOGING-IN-PUBLICATION DATA
Wheat, Carolyn.
   How to write killer fiction : the funhouse of mystery & the roller coaster of suspense /
by Carolyn Wheat.
      p. cm.
Includes bibliographical references (p.).
  ISBN 1-880284-62-6 (pbk. : alk. paper)
  1. Detective and mystery stories—Authorship. 2. Suspense fiction—Authorship. I. Title.
PN3377.5.D4 W46 2003
  808.3'872—dc21
                    2002015588

Acknowledgments

EVERYTHING I KNOW about writing I learned from...

A lot of people.

Starting where?

Do I go back to my mother, the former English teacher and born editor who helped me rewrite a seventh-grade science paper we titled "Man and His Muscles"?

Thanks, Ma. Nothing like a zippy title.

Or the first time I read a composition out loud in class and kids laughed because it was funny and they liked it and I realized that words on paper had power?

Should I thank all the nuns who drilled me on grammar, took red pencils to my too-often-overheated prose, and introduced me to great writers?

Why not? Thank you, Sisters all, even the drill sergeant whose eighth-grade classroom taught me all the grammar I'll ever need.

I thank my first agent, John Ware, and my first editor, Hope Dellon of St. Martin's Press, for taking a chance on a lawyer-turned-writer. I thank my present agent, Ellen Geiger of Curtis, Brown for following me down many a tortuous path (I still think that *Star Trek* Tarot Deck should have been a winner), and I thank Natalee Bernstein of Berkley Prime Crime for sticking with Cass Jameson and me as long as possible.

I never believed in critique groups until I was in The Best Writers Group Ever with Donald Porter, Roy Sorrells, Donna Meyer, and

K.T. Anders. Each member of the group contributed something different to the process of making our writing better, week by week.

From Katie the actress I learned to add physicality to my characters. They couldn't remain talking heads when she read your prose; she constantly asked what the bodies were doing. Donna was the fastest line editor in the world, making quick corrections with her pen while you read your sentences aloud. Roy contributed passion, always questioning whether the action was as dramatic as it could possibly be.

Donald was our leader and our chief theorist. I used to laugh at his immense collection of how-to books and his determination to break the process down the way you'd break down a car to see all the parts.

Donald's revenge: I've *become* him. I'll bet my writers' library rivals his for depth and breadth, and I now study the process with a fascination akin to what scientists feel for mapping the human genome. If there's a writing genome, Donald will be the first to map it.

I've attended a lot of workshops and heard some great speakers. I feel I learn something from every one, so it's hard to be specific in case I leave out important people. I learned to write short stories from Lynn Barrett, who taught at a wonderful summer retreat run by the International Women's Writing Guild. It was a marvelously eclectic (one of the most popular classes was juggling) weeklong celebration of creativity, and I thank Alice Harron Orr for bringing me there that first year. Lawrence Block's Write for Your Life seminars offered wonderful insights into the soul aspects of writing, and introduced me to people who became friends.

Mystery Writers of America in New York City gave me my first opportunity to teach writing. From that first four-week class, I developed a course for the New School for Social Research, and each time I taught I learned more about the process. Professor B.J. Rahn of Hunter College introduced me to some of the theoretical writings on the mystery genre; her "Murder at Hunter" conference will never be forgotten by those of us fortunate enough to attend.

I thank Sue Dunlap, Judy Greber (aka Gillian Roberts), and Marilyn Wallace for inviting me to participate in the Book Passage Mystery Writers Conference. This is one of the great writing events, and I feel privileged to have been asked back several times. Another teaching venue I've appreciated over the years is the Bare Bones Mystery Writers Conference, put on by the San Diego chapter of Sisters in Crime. I've learned so much from the many workshop presenters I've listened to at both conferences that I can't name names, but I've always been glad I came.

My two years in Oklahoma meant a great deal to me as a teacher, and I thank Carolyn G. Hart for making them possible. She informed me that the job of Artist in Residence at the University of Central Oklahoma was available, and her strong recommendation undoubtedly contributed to my being hired. I expanded my horizons there, teaching Horror Writing and Writing Realism in addition to mystery and suspense oriented courses. Thanks also to Dr. Lynnette Wert, chair of the Creative Studies Department, for her support and encouragement.

There's nothing more fun for writers than hanging around other writers, and mystery fan conventions have always fed me. I come away energized, amazed at the many paths our genre is capable of taking, and recommitted to my own work. From my first Bouchercon in 1984 to the Malice Domestic I attended during the Year of Breast Cancer to the 2002 Left Coast Crime in Portland, I've always loved the conventions and I've always felt I received more than the full measure of enjoyment and enlightenment. Quick piece of advice: for every writer's conference you attend, go to one fan convention as well. As Sharyn McCrumb once said, "Mystery is a small town, and Tony Hillerman is its mayor." So come to town. Meet the folks. Stay a while.

The great thing about writing is that teachers are everywhere, as close as the nearest book. The other great thing is that there is always something new to learn. So here's a final thank you to all the masters of the art, from whom I take inspiration and toward whom I feel respect bordering on awe.

Contents

Preface

THE BEST ADVICE on writing I've ever seen came from a fictional character. Seymour Glass, J.D. Salinger's cryptic antihero, tells his brother, Buddy, an aspiring writer: "You think of the book you'd most like to be reading, and then you sit down and shamelessly write it."

That's the essence of this insider's guide: helping the writer select the book he'd most like to be reading, then helping him identify the particular pleasures of his chosen genre in order to bring his story to life in the way most satisfying to the reader of that genre.

How To Write Killer Fiction differs from other books about writing in detailing the crucial distinction between mystery and suspense fiction in terms of the experience the reader expects from each. When choosing to enter the funhouse of mystery, the reader wants to be puzzled, to be uneasily aware that things are not what they seem, to see the world through a distorting lens, to follow along as a detective separates truth from illusion. Riding the roller coaster of suspense, the reader looks forward to being hurtled through a fast-moving set of events that leaves him breathless, feeling emotions that rocket to the sky and plunge to the depths in a matter of seconds as a hero confronts her greatest fears.

Understanding the expectations a reader brings to each genre allows the writer to create the experience the reader most enjoys.

The Funhouse of Mystery

In the mystery, whether a cozy whodunit with its focus on puzzle, or a private eye novel with its emphasis on gritty realism, the reader meets a detective who brings skill and insight to the solution of a murder. The reader identifies with a hero who is in control, who is able to see and understand what ordinary people cannot, who peels away layers of lies to reveal the buried truth.

The central problem of the mystery is not "who killed X," but who *covered up* the killing of X, and *how did he succeed in creating the illusion that he did not kill X.* It is the task of the detective to strip away the "fake reality" created by the murderer, to work her way through the funhouse, with its distortions and reflections, and put the world back in order by recreating the truth about the murder. By the end of the classic mystery, we not only know the identity of the killer but we have also unraveled lies and secrets unrelated to the murder, for the detective's job is to seek truth everywhere.

The Roller Coaster of Suspense

In contrast to the intellectual pleasure of the mystery, suspense is an emotional roller-coaster ride; if there is a puzzle element, it is decidedly secondary to the visceral experience. The suspense hero, like the protagonist of a folk or fairy tale, faces tests that will elevate him to another level of maturity. The suspense hero, unlike most detectives who already have the skills to detect, must learn skills to cope with the new reality that has overtaken him. We readers want to see him *becoming* a hero through overcoming obstacles on the way to the showdown with evil. By the end of the novel, he has walked through the fire and has emerged as a different, larger person.

Suspense comes in many packages: romantic suspense, spy novel, techno-thriller, legal thriller, political thriller—indeed, the term "thriller" is enough to convey the roller-coaster effect of a well-constructed suspense novel. We read it, not to be entertained by a detective sifting through the clues of a past murder, but to grit our teeth and bite our nails as our hero dodges bullets and evades danger in the present.

The ending of a suspense novel, like that of a mystery, must satisfy. But where the mystery satisfies its readers by being logical, complete, and believable, the suspense novel must also satisfy emotionally. Some suspense novels that disappoint do so, not because the final chapters are unsatisfactory, but because the author failed to develop the middle sufficiently to support the final act. Others give the reader a less than resonant ending by holding back, taking the characters to less than the maximum danger and confrontation. Pulling out all the stops is the only way to conclude a powerhouse suspense novel.

The Writing Process

The final section of this book concerns the writing process. Some writers need the security of an outline; they plot the entire novel either on paper or in their heads before beginning chapter one. Others thrive on the excitement of facing a blank page; they feel stifled if they know too much before they begin to write. This book honors both processes, while recognizing that each contains its own pitfalls. The Outliner may lose verve; the Blank-pager often wanders into byways that don't move the book as a whole.

I offer advice for both instinctive Outliners and natural Blank-pagers. I discuss expansion and contraction as processes that recur in cycles throughout the entire period of writing the novel. Both types of writers are expansive at the outset, casting their nets wide to bring in as many ideas as possible. The Outliner contracts the material through the outline process; the Blank-pager is more likely to finish a first draft and then begin narrowing and focusing through revision. Either writer will find suggestions and encouragement in this book, which offers hints for dealing with problems at various stages. In addition, you'll find recognition of the enormous task of writing a novel, with ideas on how to manage paper and disk, how and when to revise, and when to call it finished.

I'm the kind of person who has to know *why*. Telling me there are rules that have to be followed is not the best way to convince me of anything—yet I've become a passionate advocate of "the rules" about mystery writing. This is because I think I understand *why* a good mystery novel must contain certain elements, and because I see "the rules" as rooted firmly in the notion of what makes the mystery experience satisfying for the reader.

I believe that if a writer understands the *why* of mystery and suspense novels, he will be able to master the *how*s without too much trouble—and the writing will be enhanced by a deep understanding of the underlying psychology of the genre. This book is not about formula writing, but about an organic appreciation of story.

If anything in this book works for you, I'm glad. If it doesn't, toss it away and write from your gut, always keeping in mind the one immutable fact about fiction: You're the one creating the reader's experience.

How To
Write Killer
Fiction

Introduction

Fiction Is Like a Dream

THE LATE John Gardner wrote, "Fiction is like a dream." Like a dream, fiction can send us on a roller-coaster ride of sensation, or it can produce images as distorted as any to be seen in the funhouse mirror at the carnival. Like a dream, it can leave us vaguely hung over, unable to experience the reality of daylight, yearning instead for the mysteries and ambiguities of night. Like a dream, fiction can reach its tendrils into our waking consciousness, haunting our hours until we can return to its potent illusions.

Unlike a dream, fiction is a manufactured experience. And it is you the writer who creates the dream for your intended reader. It is vital, therefore, that you the writer understand fully the experience you intend your reader to have. Are you offering a roller-coaster ride through danger, or are you instead masterminding a trip through the funhouse, with all the distorting mirrors reflecting images that are not what they seem? It is only by knowing precisely the effect you wish to create that you can give the reader exactly what he is looking for.

Two Different Dreams

If fiction is like a dream, then suspense is a nightmare. The hero, and through the hero the reader, is plunged into chaos, driven from one extreme to the other, hounded and disbelieved and threatened with ultimate danger. How, you wonder, can this be considered an enjoyable experience, one your reader is going to eagerly embrace? Because you the writer guarantee a happy ending in which the hero will come through the nightmare a better person, and the reader will breathe a sigh of heartfelt relief. It's the literary equivalent of waking in a cold sweat, yet filled with a sense of well-being and gratitude that it was, after all, only a dream.

At the opposite pole of the popular crime fiction genre is the whodunit. Here the nightmare of sudden, violent death is tamed, put into a neat, logical package of detection and clues, rendered less frightening by the imposition of order. The detective hero, unlike the suspense hero, is the master of the situation, keeping her head when all about her are losing theirs. The detective manages the out-of-control emotions of others and brings logic and insight to bear on the puzzle of unexplained passions. Here the experience is one of taking control while the dream is going on, of telling oneself: I can handle this; it's only a dream.

In essence, then, the reader who buys a whodunit and the reader who plunks down six bucks for a suspense novel are buying two different dreams. One is a power fantasy: the Great Detective is in control, unaffected by the powerful emotions around him. The other is a victim fantasy: the hero is buffeted by the winds of fate—but she will prevail in the end, thanks to skills she hardly knew she possessed.

Reason and Emotion

Every aspect of the well-written whodunit and the well-crafted suspense novel reflects these distinct dream-experiences. In the whodunit, the reader identifies with someone outside the troubled circle where the crime takes place; whether the sleuth is a cop, a private eye, or an amateur, the classic mystery is a story of other people's troubles. In recent years, detective characters have begun solving their own personal problems in the course of the mystery, but the core of the genre is a situation involving murder that happens to other people.

In a straight suspense novel, the hero is the center of the book. The troubles are his, not someone else's. The reader identifies with the hero and goes through a catharsis by following the hero's journey every step of the way. At the end of the story, the hero, as in a fairy tale, emerges at a different level of maturity.

In suspense, the emotions are up-front and dominant. The big scenes are played out in front of the reader; we see good and evil clash before our eyes. The hero is pursued, captured, tortured in real time, while a time bomb ticks in the background. We expect to see the hero working her way free from the ropes that bind her; we will be extremely disappointed to come on the scene after she's freed herself.

In the mystery, on the other hand, the biggest scene of all, the actual murder, takes place offstage. Most of the emotions, in fact, are buried, hidden beneath façades and lies and secrets; it is the task of the detective to bring them to light. Much is told from the perspective of the present looking back upon the past. A police procedural begins with a dead body, and the living person who once existed is seen only in recollections. The private eye novel contains more violence and conflict in the present, but deep-rooted anguish often lies at the bottom of the problem. The immediacy involves the identity and apprehension of the killer, not the intense emotion that gave rise to the murder in the first place.

Two Steps Ahead, Two Steps Behind

One key to the distinction between mystery and suspense writing involves the relative positions of hero and reader. In the ideal mystery novel, the reader is two steps behind the detective. We mystery writers want our readers to smack themselves on the forehead when the murderer's identity is revealed, to say: "I should have known! If only I'd remembered that Sally used to be a nurse, I could have figured out that she had access to the digitalis."

What we don't want is a reader who says instead, "I figured that out in chapter four; why did it take this so-called Great Detective so long?" And since the death of the Golden Age, we also no longer want our reader to say, "I couldn't have figured that out in a million years, it was so complicated and far-fetched." We want our readers to stay that ideal two steps behind the detective.

The ideal suspense reader, on the other hand, is two steps ahead of the hero. "Don't go into that old, dark house tonight," the reader begs as Mary Sue puts on her coat to go meet the nice young man she met at the library earlier that day. He's promised to tell her the whole truth about her dead grandfather, but we the readers know he's up to no good. We know something she doesn't (often because the book is written in third person; more on this later), and we writhe in suspense as she steps into danger. We are two steps ahead of her—and that's precisely where the wise suspense writer wants us to be.

Myth vs. Tale

The classic mystery, whether hard- or soft-boiled, has an aura of myth about it. Sherlock Holmes has much in common with the wizards and magicians of old; Jane Marple is a wise woman—or a witch, depending on your point of view—who sees what others miss. Philip Marlowe and Travis McGee are today's knights-errant, on a quest for honor in an honorless world.

The classic Great Detective is a finished product; we don't expect character development from Nero Wolfe or Hercule Poirot. They don't change or grow because they already embody all the qualities and skills they need to do the job they were sent to earth to do.

Today's detectives may be a trifle more fallible; they may change and grow and go in and out of relationships and question their place in the universe—but when it comes to their ability to see what others miss, to peel away the masks and layers of falsehood, they still retain a mythic aura. The Just-the-facts-ma'am cop who plays no favorites, the Hard-boiled Detective in his trench coat and fedora, and the Perry Mason–like lawyer who always defends the innocent have become archetypes in their own right.

The suspense hero, on the other hand, is not born to succeed. He must learn skills; he is usually presented at the outset as having little ability to cope with the new world into which he's been thrust. The model here is more fairy tale than myth: a king had three sons, the first two of whom were the bravest and handsomest men in the kingdom. But the youngest son was called Simple, and his brothers laughed at him because he was not brave. Guess which brother is the hero. The orphaned female hero will, like Cinderella, emerge from her ordeal a fully mature woman who has earned the love of her prince.

Larger World/Smaller World

The suspense hero is thrust from a small, safe world into a larger, very dangerous one. Often, the hero spends time and energy trying to return to the safe world she knew before the adventure began. Sometimes the small, safe world of the hero is invaded by vicious messengers from a larger world, forcing the hero to adopt larger-world tactics in order to deal with them.

One of the chief pleasures of the spy/techno-thriller subgenre is that it gives the reader a passport to other countries—and the reader goes visiting, not as a tourist, but as a privileged member of the elite. We travel not just to Moscow, but to the heart of the Kremlin; we see not the usual tourist London, but the inner workings of MI5. We eavesdrop on Hitler and Roosevelt and Stalin as they discuss their forthcoming meeting at Yalta. The hero of this kind of suspense novel is a modern Cassandra; he knows and speaks truth, but he is not listened to.

The detective's world, in contrast, narrows instead of expanding. There is a small circle of suspects to be questioned; clues are often found in the tiniest of objects: a thread, a bent blade of grass, a minuscule discrepancy between one witness's story and another's. Even in the hardest of the hard-boiled mysteries, there are subterranean connections between suspects; the murder will turn out to be committed by someone we have reason to suspect, even if all the suspects aren't gathered around a drawing room for the final twenty pages.

Information Concealed or Revealed

The tension in the mystery depends on information withheld from the reader. A clue is interesting because it must be interpreted; it is not clear on its face what the red thread at the scene of the crime means. It will take the detective's brain to make the connection between the thread and the bellman's uniform worn by the clever killer, and then to put that bit of information together with some other seemingly random fact to form a chain of evidence that will convict someone of the crime.

The suspense novel relies on information given to the reader; we know that when our hero's back is turned, the old friend she's asked for help will telephone the Nazis and give away her location. She sleeps in ignorance in the best bedroom, believing herself safe at last, while the SS is on its way. We shudder with anticipation; will she wake in time to escape? How will she get out of the house? Where will she go? We are worried about her because we have been given information she doesn't have.

Central Questions

The central question of the mystery is: Who did it? Can our detective unravel the puzzle and bring the killer to justice?

The ending of the mystery is intellectually satisfying. We understand the truth of what happened, and we believe that this truth explains all that confused us in the course of the story.

Emotional satisfaction comes, first and foremost, from the fact that we accept the solution to the mystery on an intellectual level.

The central question of the suspense novel is: Will our hero survive? Will she prevail?

The ending of the suspense novel is emotionally satisfying: our hero is not only alive, she has successfully undergone an ordeal and has become a stronger person on another plane of existence. A man has become a mensch; a girl has become a woman.

A mystery novel is at its most satisfying when it is part of a series. The best way for a mystery writer to create growth in a detective character is to do it over a series of books; the focus of each separate story is still the solution of an individual crime. The detective hero ends or begins a relationship, comes to terms with her past, or faces a tough professional choice—but her personal dilemma is a subplot, subordinated to the central issue of who killed the victim.

The suspense novel can be a stand-alone book; the writer has taken the hero through a life-transforming ordeal—and this can only happen once in a lifetime. Since this hero will be seen between the covers of a book only once, the writer pulls out all the stops and tells all aspects of his story. This is especially true of the suspense novel that ends with the hero becoming a mensch; suspense stories that revolve around a hero who is already a mensch give a different kind of pleasure, a pleasure which may be repeated more than once.

Crossovers

Are there books that succeed as both a mystery and a suspense novel at the same time? *Presumed Innocent,* by Scott Turow, comes as close as any book I've ever read to doing just that.

How?

First: the mystery was solid. It was complex enough to satisfy a mystery fan; it had clues and suspects and red herrings—all the things a whodunit aficionado is looking for in a good read. Turow took the reader into the funhouse of mystery, showing us distorted images and confusing pictures of what might have been until we were just as befuddled as he wanted us to be.

Second: the hero was in personal danger, not from a villain out to kill him, but from the legal system that put him on trial for killing his lover. Turow took us on the roller-coaster ride that is the hallmark of suspense; one chapter we were up, we felt Rusty was innocent and was going to win his case; the next chapter we were convinced he was on his way to the chair—and what was more, we believed he deserved to be.

Both the mystery and suspense aspects of the book were given equal weight in the writing—and that's not something most writers in the genre can pull off. One thing that helped Turow is the intellectual nature of criminal trials. He wasn't trying to balance the essentially cerebral function of detection with physical derring-do; instead, the detective/suspense hero's skills as a lawyer were tested to the full by the courtroom battle.

Another road to crossover success is the one paved by Elizabeth George, whose *A Traitor to Memory* weighs in at a hefty 710 pages. This length comes about because George is literally writing two books in one: a straightforward police procedural mystery about a death in the present day, and a psychological suspense novel centering on events from the distant as well as the recent past. The result is a kaleidoscope of plot, subplot, sub-sub-plot, character arcs, turns and twists, emotional resonance—it's a book you fall into and emerge from a week later, blinking at the light as if you'd been in a cave. Its 710 pages are the result of an intensely disciplined writing mind, and Ms. George wrote at this length only after publishing shorter books.

My advice to beginning writers who want to write the next best-selling crossover book: Don't. My advice is to stick to one side or the other of the equation, to go into the funhouse or to step on the roller coaster and not try for both in the same book. It can be done, but it's difficult. And the reason it's difficult is that you are combining two different dreams.

There are suspense elements in many mysteries, and some top-notch suspense writers add mystery elements to their plotlines, but this is not the same as attempting a true crossover. Writing two books in one is a very difficult proposition, and one that demands an almost obsessive attention to structure.

Different Dreams, Different Choices

So enter the funhouse of mystery and see how the twists and turns of the mazelike passageways disorient you. Move on to the roller coaster and take the plunge into terror. Then decide which you enjoyed more, and choose that experience as the main focus of your book.

The rest of this book will explore the ways the writer makes the dream happen for the reader; it will follow the distinction between suspense and mystery, detailing the specific techniques that will best create each kind of dream. And it will discuss how to switch gears from mystery to suspense in order to add spice to the mystery, and how to plant mystery elements in the suspense novel that will add to its intellectual enjoyment.

Write What You Read

Who's your favorite author, the one you turn to after a hard day at work, a day spent with three kids down with chicken pox, a day of dreary drizzle? Is it a classic whodunit in modern dress, a Carolyn G. Hart, a Margaret Maron, a Robert Barnard? Or is it a hard-boiled private eye—a Grafton, a Pronzini, a Paretsky, a Robert B. Parker? It could be that police or forensic procedurals like those of Patricia Cornwell, Ed McBain, or Kathy Reichs are your security-blanket reads.

Or is suspense your favorite escape? Perhaps Mary Higgins Clark, Barbara Michaels, or Dick Francis sweeps you away. Or maybe it's the techno or legal side of the thriller, with Clancy or Grisham, Crichton or Ludlum. Maybe it's the potent mix of suspense and mystery, as delivered by Jonathan Kellerman, T. Jefferson Parker, or Elizabeth George.

The major reason to identify your favorite kind of book is so you can read like a writer. As you read your favorite author, ask yourself what it is about the book that brings you into the story, what keeps you turning the page. Identify the particular pleasures of the book, and try to figure out exactly how the writer created those pleasures on the page. When you come to write your own novel, you'll find that the techniques your favorite writer used are accessible to you as well.

Mystery/Suspense Checklist

Mystery	Suspense
puzzle	nightmare
power fantasy	victim fantasy
myth	fairy tale
detective has skills	hero learns skills
thinking paramount	feeling paramount
action offstage	action onstage
small circle of suspects	hero's world enlarges
clues	surprises
information withheld	information given
reader two steps behind	reader two steps ahead
who killed X?	will hero prevail?
suspects	betrayers
red herrings	cycles of distrust
satisfaction: intellectual	satisfaction: emotional

Part 1:
The Funhouse
of Mystery

1. Welcome to the Funhouse

What Is a Mystery Novel?

WE ENTER the funhouse of mystery, and the first question many ask themselves is: What the heck is a funhouse?

Ah, youth. Sometimes called the Crazy House, the funhouse was a mainstay of old-fashioned carnivals and midways, the kind of amusement parks people went to before Walt Disney discovered Anaheim. Check out some old newsreel footage of Coney Island if you want the full picture, and this is what you'll see:

Welcome to the Funhouse _____

It's dark inside. You enter through a giant clown's head with an open mouth that becomes a door. Once inside, things happen without warning. You turn a corner and a skeleton pops out of the wall, stopping inches from your face. Maniacal laughter comes out of nowhere, and blasts of cold air meet you when you enter another corridor.

Nothing is what it seems. You're in a maze, where a wrong turn leads you to a blind alley, a dead end. You encounter floors that move unexpectedly, shift and tilt and have you sliding backwards, grabbing at the walls. Skulls on springs jump at you and taunting Joker-like voices dare you to take the next pathway.

You walk into the hall of mirrors and become part of the entertainment. Distorting mirrors make you look like a plump dwarf one minute, a skinny giant the next. Rows of mirrors one after another create an infinity effect that makes it seem as if you'll never get out of the fun-house, that you might be trapped in a place of dangerous illusion forever. When you want to leave, you're led down corridors that go nowhere, di-verted back to where you've already been, guided through a maze that ends (at least this is how it ended at my childhood amusement park, Sandusky's Cedar Point) with a huge polished wooden slide. Attendants give you a tiny rug to sit on and then push you down, down, down the slick surface to the ground floor and out into the sunlight where you blink as if you've been inside for a week.

What does this have to do with murder mysteries?

It's been forty years or more since I experienced the Cedar Point fun-house (for some reason, they just don't exist anymore, not the way they used to), and it still remains in my mind the most powerful metaphor I can think of for the well-plotted detective story. Things come out of the blue; the detective walks down dead-end pathways and finds the truth obscured by distractions and distortions. Even the detective herself seems distorted, changed, by the act of investigating the crime.

Just when the detective thinks she has it all figured out, someone puts her on a slick slide to nowheresville, and she's back on the street with nothing.

A Little Mystery History

The idea of the detective all but preceded the reality. Mystery's founding father, Edgar Allan Poe, set his 1841 short story "The Murders in the Rue Morgue" in Paris because Paris, unlike most major cities of the day, actually had a police force with a detective division. Poe called his story "a tale of ratiocination" and introduced the amateur detective who reasoned rings around the official police investigator, bringing logic and science to bear on the problem of crime.

In Poe's stories and in Sir Arthur Conan Doyle's Sherlock Holmes adventures, the amateur detectives use scientific methods, while the po-lice prefer using street informers and beating confessions out of the usual suspects. The detectives, C. Auguste Dupin and Sherlock Holmes, are the ones on their knees picking up threads and hairs, and they see beyond the obvious in ways the stolid, less-educated police detectives can't.

Poe bequeathed the mystery writer two very important principles: "the impossible made possible"—the Locked Room Mystery (as exemplified by "The Murders in the Rue Morgue"), and "the obvious made obscure" ("The Purloined Letter.")

These principles embody the funhouse experience: What you see is most emphatically not what you get. In "The Murders in the Rue Morgue," we're introduced to the first of many fictional murders that seem inexplicable. The room is locked; the windows are high and too small for a person to have entered. Yet there are dead bodies inside; the thing happened even though it couldn't possibly have happened.

The police are baffled—and baffled police are always good for the amateur detective—because they can't, in that most nineties of clichés, think outside the box. A person couldn't have scaled the walls and entered the room—but what if the murderer *isn't* a person? (No, we're not talking supernatural agencies here; if you don't know who committed the murders in the Rue Morgue, find a collection of Poe stories, because some things you have to experience for yourself.)

Locked Room Mysteries aren't the only venue for the "impossible made possible" strain of mystery plot construction. Any murderer who fakes an alibi is creating an "impossible" situation—nobody can be in two places at once—and making it "possible." In the same vein, a killer who creates the illusion that his victim is alive after the murder has been committed also makes the impossible possible.

The second principle, "the obvious made obscure," is another linchpin of the detective story. In "The Purloined Letter," Dupin is called in when the French police fail to find an important letter they know is hidden in an apartment. They've lifted floorboards and axed into walls, they've taken apart the stove and looked inside every book in the library, but they haven't looked in the one place that seems too obvious, too stupid, too mindless to constitute a successful hiding place.

"Hide in plain sight" will be one of the main methods of clue concealment we'll discuss later in this book. It's your job as the mystery writer to create clues leading to the identity of the murderer and then to conceal those clues in a way that fools the reader without making a fool of him.

That Was Then, This Is Now

"Okay, so Edgar Allan Poe invented the detective story and got an award named after him. What does that have to do with my writing a mystery novel in the twenty-first century?"

Plenty, if only because that original template for the tale of detection is imprinted on the brains of everyone who ever reached for a library book because it had a little red skull stamped on the spine. The mystery reader opens a book with certain expectations, and the writer who knows what those expectations are can give the reader what she wants in a way that delights and surprises her.

What's happened to the mystery since Holmes hung up his deerstalker and started keeping bees? For one thing, it split into three distinct strands, all of which are still very much in evidence on the bookstore shelves.

The Classic Whodunit

Poet and mystery reader W.H. Auden called it "the dialectic of innocence and guilt." Today's fans call it the "cozy," meaning no disrespect but expressing perfectly that feeling readers of the traditional mystery get when they pick up a new whodunit, go home and make tea, and wrap themselves in a physical quilt as well as the metaphoric quilt of a story they know will have a happy ending.

The happy ending—okay, "happy" may be going too far—the *positive* ending, the ending that brings justice to bear on a violent situation, the ending where reason triumphs over evil; that's the ending classic readers are looking for.

Why? Because ever since Poe, the classic tale of detection has meant restoring order to a world that was once well ordered but lost that serenity through violent death.

Auden calls the scene of the crime before the murder is committed "the great good place." It is the English village, the manor house, the theater, the university, the monastery, any place that thrives upon stability and hierarchy. Into this idyllic world step not one, but *two* undesirables: the killer and her victim. The killer rids the great good place of the victim; it's up to the detective to flush out and remove the murderer and restore goodness.

Subgenres of the traditional mystery include:

The Regional Mystery

The old-time traditional whodunit placed little emphasis on setting except insofar as it furthered the puzzle itself. The grand country house could be in any part of England, the sinister university or the bedeviled theater could be anywhere in Britain, the U.S., or New Zealand—we weren't reading for a travelogue or for insight into local culture.

Tony Hillerman helped to change all that. His mysteries took place on Navajo lands, and the land itself was a major factor in creating the circumstances and the means for murder. The people and their culture were important to the solution of the mystery, which could not have been solved by an outsider without knowledge of Navajo myth and mindset. Even though Hillerman's detectives were police officers, the experience of reading about an exotic place and seeing it through the eyes of someone with deep understanding of the place and its people whetted mystery readers' appetites for more of the same, only different.

When Margaret Maron wrote *The Bootlegger's Daughter*, her first Deborah Knott mystery, she changed her setting from the New York City of her Sigrid Harald police procedurals to the rich soil of North Carolina, sweeping that year's awards in the process. Soon mysteries were set in Alaska (Dana Stabenow, Sue Henry, John Straley), in national parks (Nevada Barr), and in the formerly hidden world of Orthodox Jewry in New York and Los Angeles (Faye Kellerman, Rochelle Krich). More and more writers found Native American connections and set their books among the Cherokee (Jean Hager), the Arapaho (Margaret Coel), the Ute (James Doss), and the Pima (J.A. Jance).

The keys to writing a successful regional mystery are choosing a region interesting enough to engage the reader and making sure the mystery itself isn't swamped by description and portraits of local eccentrics. Those of us unlucky enough not to have grown up in the Alaska bush or the Louisiana bayou have another option: turn back the clock.

The Historical Mystery

"The past is a foreign country," L.P. Hartley wrote in *The Go-Between*. "They do things differently there." Using an exotic setting for your traditional mystery may involve choosing a location you can't get to by train or plane. Through mysteries, you can visit ancient Egypt (Lynda Robinson), ancient Rome (Steven Saylor, Lindsey Davis), Victorian England (Anne Perry), the 1920s (Annette Meyers, Carola Dunn), medieval Europe (Sharan Newman, Ellis Peters). You can meet historic figures such as Houdini (Barbara Michaels, Daniel Stashower, Walter Satterthwaite), the Prince of Wales (not the current one; Queen Victoria's oldest son) (Peter Lovesey), or Jane Austen (Stephanie Barron).

Some authors choose history because they love a certain period and want to share their deep understanding of it with readers. Others frankly admit that one of the charms of history is that it lacks DNA testing. In a world without modern forensics, the amateur, be he monk or prince, has as good a chance of success as the official investigating body. By removing today's scientifically inclined police from the scene, they essentially recreate the conditions under which Dupin and Holmes first flourished.

Comic Relief

Playing it for laughs has been part of the mystery tradition even before Craig Rice, the screwball comedy queen of the forties, and humor spans all three of the major subgenres. Joan Hess combines humor and regionalism in her Maggody series, while Parnell Hall injects hearty doses of laughter into his Stanley Hastings P.I. series. For a wonderful sendup of the old country house mystery, James Anderson's *Affair of the Blood-stained Egg Cosy* is a must, while Lawrence Block's more recent Bernie Rhodenbarr books give us sly variations on some of the oldest tricks in the traditional mystery book.

The only caveat about using humor: to paraphrase the old actor's saying, "Killing people is easy; comedy is hard."

You Gotta Have a Gimmick

Take a stroll through your local bookstore to check out the mystery shelves and you'll see what I mean by a gimmick. If talking cats (Carole Nelson Douglas, Rita Mae Brown) aren't solving crimes, then cooks who provide the reader with recipes do the job (Diane Mott Davidson, Jerrilyn Farmer). Herbalist-detectives (Susan Wittig Albert) give advice on how to dry and use oregano, while crossword puzzle mysteries (Parnell Hall) provide double the pleasure for the word addict. Some of the strictest rules of the old school are broken by authors using ghosts (Nancy Atherton's *Aunt Dimity's Death*) and psychics (Martha Lawrence's Elizabeth Chase series) as detectives.

The trick is not to allow the gimmick to replace a solid mystery core. The culinary detective must not only cook, she must detect. The psychic detective must do more than just wait for inspiration from the beyond.

The "Dark Cozy"

The classic whodunit has been called a comedy of manners, but in

America, broader social commentary has been part of the genre ever since Mark Twain's *Pudd'nhead Wilson*, the first book ever to use fingerprints as a mode of detection (well before their use crept into real-life police work). Today's traditional mysteries go deeper than the Golden Age writers ever thought about going and today's writers use the form to explore social and personal problems.

Nancy Pickard deals with mental illness in *I.O.U.* Margaret Maron examines the bitter heritage of Southern racism in *Home Fires*. Minette Walters (*The Ice House*) delves deeply into the psychological torment beneath placid middle-class façades.

It may even seem that the traditional lines have blurred. There are cozies that bite and private eyes who cry.

The American Hard-Boiled Detective Story

If Agatha Christie's St. Mary Mead is "the great good place," as Auden insists, then the American urban landscape constitutes "the great wrong place." This is the San Francisco of Dashiell Hammett's Sam Spade, the Los Angeles of Raymond Chandler and Ross Macdonald, the Florida of Elmore Leonard, the New York of Lawrence Block's Matt Scudder.

In this world, murder is not an aberration. Order didn't exist before this particular victim was killed, and it's not going to exist after the killer is caught. Justice isn't really possible; the most you can get is "some justice."

"It's Chinatown, Jake," Gittes's cop pal reminds him at the end of *Chinatown*, when it's clear that the villain will get away with his crimes, and the point is that it's *all* Chinatown. In this world, the cops aren't amiable bunglers; they're corrupt and actively hostile to any truth that could upset the rotten apple cart. Even if the killer is hauled away in handcuffs or blown away by a well-aimed .44, the idyllic, peaceful, orderly world represented by the English village is very, very far away.

This world demands a different detective from the cerebral, scientific Great Detective. An investigator going head-to-head with a villain this violent had better be able to use violence himself if necessary. The scientific method isn't much use if the evidence will never see the inside of a courtroom because the cops are corrupt and won't arrest anyone with too much power. Other qualities are called for in this type of mystery, and the hard-boiled detective embodies those traits.

Yes, I'm going to quote Chandler. Here it comes: "Down these mean streets a man must go who is not himself mean, who is neither tarnished nor afraid." That phrase lies at the heart of the American hard-boiled tradition, and it's as alive in Sue Grafton's Kinsey Millhone and Walter Mosley's Easy Rawlins as it ever was in the old *Black Mask* days.

Tough private eyes started out as white American males. Women were faithful, warmhearted secretaries, long-suffering girlfriends, and red-lipsticked *femmes fatales*. Nonwhite males and females appeared as walk-on characters at best. Today's shamuses come in both genders and all races. The great wrong place is no longer just the American city; a sense that officialdom can be bought pervades the world. Justice is hard to come by, as some sensational jury verdicts have shown, and the sensibility of the private eye reflects that cynical approach to reality.

With the widening of the circle, new perspectives entered the field. It's all but impossible to read books set in Los Angeles during the forties and fifties without filtering them through Walter Mosley's Easy Rawlins series, which illuminates the dark heart of racism that permeated the LAPD. V.I. Warshawski and Kinsey Millhone walk those mean streets with the same incorruptible courage shown by Philip Marlowe, yet because they're female they bring a different sensibility to the art of private investigation. Marcus Didius Falco wears a toga instead of a trench coat, but his anachronistic presence in ancient Rome allows us to see that long-dead world through very modern eyes.

Non-P.I. detectives who act like private eyes even though they wear a badge (Michael Connelly's Harry Bosch, Ian Rankin's John Rebus) or have a law degree (John Lescroart's Dismas Hardy) or do social work (Abigail Padgett's Bo Bradley) provide another twist on the hard-boiled genre. It's the worldview that makes a hard-boiled story, not the fedora. It's the attitude that Harlan Coben's Myron Bolitar, sports agent, brings to his cases that makes him an integral part of this subgenre.

The essential whodunit bones are still there, but with a twist. The hard-boiled story provides us with bodies, not just a single body. Instead of the small circle of suspects being confined to a small community, there are subterranean connections between the victim and perpetrator that the detective must uncover. The villains make active attempts to silence the detective by force rather than throw him off the scent with false clues. A world of random violence instead of stability leads to the impossibility of restoring order to a place that never had order to begin with.

The Procedural

Somewhere along the line, mystery writers realized that murders weren't actually being solved by gifted amateurs with independent incomes or by seedy private eyes with bottles of rye whiskey in their desk drawers. Real cops did real work and, at least occasionally, came up with the killer. Like Sherlock Holmes, these detectives used science, like the Hard-boiled Dicks, they used violence when necessary. Unlike the cops in St. Mary Mead, they weren't bunglers; unlike the cops in Bay City, California, they weren't corrupt.

The antecedents of the classic whodunit and the hard-boiled detective story are both fairly clear, but who invented the police procedural is shrouded in mystery. Was Sergeant Cuff of Wilkie Collins's *The Moonstone* (1868) the first fictional cop we readers were meant to identify with and view as a real detective? Or was it Sergeant Friday of the LAPD who galvanized mystery buffs into finally giving official police their due?

One major difference between the traditional police procedural and the other two strains of detective story is that the police are not loners. One individual does not solve the crime in a vacuum; it takes a squad, working together and sharing information, to do the job. Ed McBain's wildly successful 87th Precinct books are the perfect example; the precinct is the star, not a single detective. Reginald Hill's British procedurals center on Superintendent Andy Dalziel and his subordinates Chief Inspector Peter Pascoe and Sergeant Wield. They each interrogate different witnesses and provide pieces of the final solution to the crime, as well as bringing very different sensibilities to bear on the event.

The police solve crimes the old-fashioned way: by wearing out shoe leather canvassing witnesses and comparing their stories, by using science to connect fragments of evidence to a particular suspect, and by exploiting the power to arrest. The reader goes along for the ride because he is fascinated by the actual details of crime solving, not just the intellectual pyrotechnics of the Great Detective or the tough-guy tricks of the Hard-boiled Dick.

The procedural celebrated the police, but it also whitewashed them (pun intended). They were cast in the mold of Sgt. Joe Friday, speaking in terse syllables and devoted to justice for all. Surely there were no racists in Friday's police department, surely no one working with him ever abused a suspect or coerced a confession or planted evidence or hushed up a crime because a perpetrator was politically connected. Friday and his partners didn't even use bad language, and not only because they were television cops and had to pass the censors. They were straight-arrow stand-up guys with all the emotional depth of wood.

Joseph Wambaugh, though not a mystery writer in his early years, broke down the blue wall and let the reader see a more realistic police force. His cops weren't super-detectives, they were a mixture of profane, scared, macho, racist, compassionate, alcoholic, ambitious, burned out, loyal, and human. Above all, they were human.

James Ellroy went farther than Wambaugh in portraying the LAPD of the fifties as corrupt, violent, racist, and cunning—from top to bottom. Walter Mosley, writing a private eye series, nevertheless shone a harsh spotlight on institutional racism.

Today's police mysteries are not all procedurals. Some who detect under the auspices of police departments are actually loner private-eye characters with a badge; others are traditional detectives using traditional methods of detecting. But all bear some mark of Wambaugh's influence, because all now acknowledge that police forces and the men and women who work in them are far from perfect.

The biggest news in the world of procedurals is that they aren't confined to police anymore. Patricia Cornwell and Kathy Reichs hit the best-seller's list with medical examiner procedurals, which track the day-to-day efforts of today's forensic scientists to solve complex murder cases. Television's *CSI* takes us behind the scenes of a big-city crime scene unit and makes the most minute, painstaking matching of hairs and fibers seem like an adventure.

Other People's Troubles

Perhaps the major alteration in the world of the mystery novel was the gradual shift from the detective's concentration on other people's troubles to the present-day expectation readers have that the detective, whether amateur, private eye, or police officer, will grow and develop in the course of solving the crime.

Sherlock Holmes, Miss Marple, Nero Wolfe, Lew Archer, Perry Mason—these characters remained the same from the first day they appeared in print until their last story. Even in cases where they professed to have a strong personal connection to a victim or suspect, they didn't experience the kind of anguish today's detectives go through. The focus was on the case itself and the people involved in the case; the detective was an outsider whose essential core remained untouched. Some of them didn't even age (Hercule Poirot must have been 110 by the time he "died").

Whether your detective is a librarian who solves crimes on the side, a homicide detective on an Indian reservation, or a big-city private eye, she will probably go through more personal changes than the classic detectives named above.

Why? Because that's what today's readers are looking for. "Other people's troubles" were enough for Lew Archer, whose creator saw him as a transparent window through which he could examine the social structure of Southern California society. Today's readers want more about the detective's inner struggles and outer realities. They expect to see growth and change from one book to the next, and some level of acknowledgment of the effect past events had on the character's development to date.

Some mystery writers are producing books that are as much novels as detective stories. Minette Walters, Val McDermid, and Elizabeth George are some of the authors whose books cross genre lines into mainstream. Sarah Smith and James Ellroy (in his later books) are two whose novels are crime-based but whose sales transcend the usual genre expectations.

Write What You Read

Whom do you love? If your finished book were to be favorably compared to the work of another writer, who would you want that writer to be? This is a vital question, and something the aspiring writer should start thinking about as soon as possible, because how can you hit a target if you don't know where the target is?

Writing what you read means reading critically. It means trying to figure out, if you don't already know, exactly what it is you love about the books you love. Is it the character development, or do really tricky plots appeal to you? Are you someone who falls in love with exotic locations? Is humor essential to your ideal of a great book? Whatever wins your heart as a reader is what you need to write, because you will know by instinct and long years of loving exactly what it is that your ideal reader wants from you, and you can give it freely, without sweat or second-guessing.

2. Cover-Ups and Clues

Basic Ingredients of the Mystery

"IT'S NOT the crime, it's the cover-up." This isn't just a Washington truism; it's the essence of the novel of detection. The killer kills, and even if we the readers see the death itself, we have not seen the murder. The most significant action of the entire book takes place offstage.

What do I mean by that?

Cover-ups

Picture the scene: the English country house, the greedy relatives gathered around the dinner table while Uncle Sebastian, the rich patriarch, lifts his glass of port to his lips. He drinks, he cries out and grabs his throat. Choking and gagging, he falls to the floor and within minutes is dead as a doornail, the scent of bitter almonds on his blue lips.

We saw the death. We did not see the murder, for we didn't see the killer putting poison into the wine bottle or smearing it around the edges of the wineglass. Or, if we did, we saw a shadowy figure creep into the study and lift the port from its accustomed place. We saw a hand reach out to take the special glass that only Uncle Sebastian used. We *did not see* whose hand it was, because that would give away the game.

Cover-Up One: It Wasn't Murder

The killer kills, but not wanting to be caught, he conceals his identity. He may also choose to conceal the fact of murder itself. Thus many mysteries begin with a death the police refuse to classify as murder.

"It couldn't have been suicide—she never took pills!"

"She couldn't have drowned! She was an Olympic-level swimmer!"

"Dead! He's not dead, he's in Borneo."

The killer has killed, but he has created a cover story that results in the police refusing to investigate the death as a crime. The detective's first act of detection, then, is to discover *and prove* that the death was deliberate murder.

This is a wonderful device for the amateur detective, since it gets the police out of the way and allows the detective free rein, at least for a while. It also gives the detective a realm of investigation that doesn't directly focus on specific suspects, meaning the investigation has two distinct parts: the "was it murder" section, and the "whodunit" section. Since the big bad middle of any book is a challenge to fill, this is a great way to make sure there's enough material to go around.

An interesting variant on this is the Murder-that-isn't-a-murder. Here we have someone missing, presumed dead, presumed murdered, but either we have no body or we have a body that's been misidentified. This time the detective's job is the opposite: to prove that a death the police think is the murder of Sir George is really the death of a transient, while Sir George is alive and well and drinking margaritas in Cabo San Lucas.

The Wrong Murder is another useful device. In this gambit, some poor soul ends up dead and the police spend several chapters hunting down people with a motive to kill that individual, whereas our detective realizes that the murder was a mistake and the intended victim is still walking around and still vulnerable. (Whenever a mystery reader sees a character putting on someone else's coat, little bells go off in our heads and we're ready to bet that a Wrong Murder is about to be committed.)

What all of these devices do is clear the way for a non-police detective to investigate an aspect of the case that the police aren't interested in. The amateur can establish her detective credentials by first proving that the death was murder before embarking on the larger task of bringing the killer to justice.

Cover-Up Two: Some Other Dude Did It

The second murderer's trick is to allow the death to look like murder and to frame someone else for the crime. Now the police are in the act from the outset, so the killer must divert suspicion from herself and plant clues leading to another. (Of course, once the cops in the earlier situations realize the death is murder, the killer needs a backup plan that will involve the same things.)

Back when I worked for the Legal Aid Society in Brooklyn, we called this the Two-Dude Defense, or Some Other Dude Did It. It was purely amazing how many guys in Brooklyn were just standing on street corners chillin' when "two dudes" ran up and shoved a loaded gun or a stolen radio into their innocent hands. Before they had time to think, the cops rolled up on them and caught them red-handed.

My clients in Brooklyn seldom got away with the SODDI defense, but your murderer will give the cops a good run for their money with it. The killer not only kills, not only conceals his own guilt, but *actively plans to have someone else take the fall.*

One important element of all these approaches to the cover-up is that the murderer is not a passive observer of the detective's actions. She is plotting against the detective every step of the way, playing a high-stakes game of chess, shoving clues in front of the detective to divert suspicion away from her and toward another suspect.

Real Reality and False Reality

The murderer creates the reality of a dead body, and then creates a "false reality" to cover it up. For a long time, the detective, like the police and the other characters, sees only the "false reality." Gradually, through investigation, the detective is able to separate the truth from the fabrication.

This is the funhouse part. Like the funhouse at the old-fashioned amusement park, we encounter mirrors that distort images, passageways that lead us down blind alleys, surprises that pop out at us from seemingly uninhabited places, and misdirection designed to keep us walking around in circles. The detective is just as baffled as the official police—at first.

The "false reality" usually has two parts: the minimization of the killer's motive, opportunity, or access to means; and the maximization of someone else's motive, opportunity, or access to means.

Starting with the first of these, the killer works hard to conceal her motive to kill Uncle Sebastian. She pretends she has money of her own, so no one knows she's waiting as eagerly as everyone else for the old coot to die and leave her a legacy. She pretends to have forgiven him for stopping her marriage to the unsuitable suitor. At the same time, she takes great pains to remind everyone, including the police, that her brother needs money, that her mother never forgave Uncle S. for what he said to her last Boxing Day.

But that's just motive, and that's not enough to put the noose around someone's neck. Our killer needs to create the illusion that she *couldn't have killed* her uncle, no matter how much motive she had. Then she needs to show the police that other people could have done it, and in fact, left clues behind telling the world that they did do it.

A great many of the Golden Age detective stories depend upon alibis, for an ironclad alibi is the best way in the world to prove you couldn't possibly be the killer. Show the police you were in Detroit on the fatal day and they can't nail you for a death in Philadelphia. Show them you were receiving an award from the mayor at the time the victim was shot, and they'll have to look for someone else as the killer.

Thing is, you the writer have to figure out just how someone *can* commit murder and then make it look as if they were somewhere else at the time. You have to put yourself in the killer's shoes.

The Straight-Line Narrative

The late California crime writer Collin Wilcox called this "the idiot plot," but, believe me, it isn't for idiots. Anyone who wants to craft a sound, tight, well-constructed mystery is advised to write the crime *from the murderer's point of view.* In other words, the writer first creates "the real reality" and then creates the "false reality" that the killer uses to cover her tracks.

Let's take Uncle Sebastian's poisoning as an example. Let's say that his niece Wanda committed the crime. Here's how a straight-line narrative starring Wanda might look:

Wanda lives with her Uncle Sebastian, a cold, cruel man who treats her very badly and makes fun of her mousy looks. She accepts this until she meets a man named Hosmer Angel, who wants to marry her but worries about having enough money to start his own business. Wanda assures him she'll inherit enough money for both of them, but then Uncle Sebastian finds out about Hosmer and says he'll cut her out of his will if she even thinks about marrying him.

The Real Reality

In fact, Uncle S. announces his intention to change his will and invites his whole family to his house for his seventy-fifth birthday party. The family includes Wanda's ne'er-do-well brother Waldo, who always has his hand out for Uncle's money, her flighty sister Winnie, who wants a thousand pounds to open a dress shop, and her mother Wilhelmina, who depends upon Sebastian's generous allowance to maintain her home in Torquay. So the house is nicely stocked with suspects and we're not even counting the butler and cook, who have plans for their inheritances as well.

Uncle S. likes his port. No one else in the house drinks port. Uncle is sure to pour a glass for himself on the night of his birthday, so Wanda takes four buses to a village where she isn't known and buys a bottle of poison containing cyanide. (That means: now Wanda has what it takes to commit the murder, and she's concealed the fact that she bought it by going where she wasn't known and signing a fake name in the chemist's poison book.)

Now she has to get into Uncle Sebastian's private study, a room he keeps locked. Only the housekeeper, Mrs. Strange, has a key; she unlocks the room every Thursday for a quick dusting. So how is Wanda going to get into the room to put the poison into the port?

Answer: maybe she isn't. Maybe the port itself isn't really poisoned, but the inability of anyone to get into the study becomes a red herring. Maybe she doctors the glass Uncle Sebastian uses instead; she has access to that pretty readily. She can then divert the police by adding more poison to the decanter afterwards to make it look as if the poison was there all along.

Let's say she does get into the study by diverting Mrs. Strange after she's opened the door on Thursday. Mrs. Strange's later recollection that a salesman called at the door and asked to speak to her will explain how the room was unguarded for a short time. That the young man looks a lot like Hosmer Angel will eventually put the noose around both their necks—and you developed the clue by realizing you had to figure out a way to get Wanda into that study.

Now Wanda has not only means but opportunity as well. She's done a nice job of concealing her motive; no one else in the house knows she's seeing Hosmer Angel and wants money so she can marry him.

The False Reality

That's the real reality. Now she has to create the false reality that someone else in the house also has means and opportunity. Motive is pretty well out there already, and it looks to Inspector Dim like everyone in the house except Wanda had reasons for wanting the old boy dead (which, if he were an experienced mystery reader, would be a giant clue right there, but that's why we need Lord Bright on the case).

How does Wanda do this? Here are a few possibilities:

- She hides the bottle of cyanide in sister Winnie's sponge bag.

- She tells the inspector she saw her mother outside Uncle Sebastian's study late one night. What she doesn't say is that her mother received a note, purporting to be from Uncle S., asking her to meet him there. When Wilhelmina is asked to produce the note, she can't—because Wanda urged her to toss it into the fire.

- She mentions that brother Waldo is an amateur photographer. When the inspector checks out his darkroom, he finds cyanide.

- She points out, helpfully, that the butler's pantry contains a nice big jar of silver polish—containing cyanide. It will also appear that the butler desperately needs money because he lost a bundle on the horses.

Now she's given everyone else means and/or opportunity. She's created her false reality (of course, she'd have been better off concentrating on one suspect and putting him firmly in the frame, which is what you'll do in your straight-line narrative).

Getting a Clue _____

Mystery writing is a sadistic little craft. First we create clues for our readers to pick up, and then we do our best to obscure those clues. As Golden Age guru S.S. Van Dine said, "The really good detective story is a kind of literary game. It is more—it is a sporting event. And the author must play fair with the reader."

The play-fair mystery allows the reader to investigate along with the detective, learning exactly what the detective learns when he learns it. To quote Van Dine again, "No wilful (sic) tricks or deceptions may be played on the reader *other than those played legitimately by the criminal on the detective himself.*" Playing fair adds the pleasure of solving a puzzle to the other joys of reading fiction, such as identifying with great characters and visiting an exciting setting.

A suspense novel, as we'll see in Part Two of this book, is a different matter. While mini-mysteries and puzzles are often included in suspense reads, the writer doesn't have to play fair in order to enchant the reader. The main character in a suspense novel can keep secrets from the reader, while we expect the detective in a mystery to share with us every single clue she comes upon.

Hide in Plain Sight

When is a clue not a clue? When it is exposed to the reader *before* the crime is committed. This is a great way to convey a big fat piece of information that would have the reader saying, "It must have been Henry!" if the reader learned it after the body was discovered. But learning on page 20 that some guy named Henry once worked for a chemical company means nothing; it's only after someone is found dead of toxic fumes 70 pages later that this information becomes important.

Other great ways to hide clues:

- Toss the clue in as a throwaway line during an argument. "And that's another thing, George, you've been away three weekends in a row!" will, with luck, have us focused on George's shortcomings as a husband, not on the fact that he wasn't with Alice on the day Bruce was killed.

- Humor is another good hiding place. That reference to Henry's working for the chemical company might be inserted into a joke, and the reader will assume the information isn't meant seriously.

- One of Dame Agatha Christie's favorite methods of clue concealment was the Unreliable Narrator. Put the vital clue in the mouth of someone we know is a liar or a dolt and we're likely to discount it. But once in a while, a liar tells the truth and a dolt gets an insight.

- Half truths are still lies—but the reader is likely to think he's received the whole truth and forget to question what was left unsaid.

- Second cousin to the Unreliable Narrator is the Prattler, a character whose mouth is always open and always dispensing trivial talk that no one listens to. After a while, the reader stops paying attention, too—and that's the point at which you put something important into that character's mouth.

- A personal favorite: give the reader one nice big clue and then shove another one in after it. Let the first clue shine brightly, so that it attracts the reader, who picks it up, pats him/herself on the back, and assumes that nothing else in that sentence or paragraph is a clue because they've already sucked the meat out of that walnut.

- Along the same lines, how about giving the reader a clue that the detective immediately recognizes as such, and then coming up with a secondary meaning for that clue, which now makes it point in a completely different direction. A word that seems to have one meaning suddenly takes on a new connotation and points the detective in a different direction.

The Dog in the Night-Time

The absence of a clue can become a clue, as in "the dog in the night-time." The reference is from "Silver Blaze," in which Sherlock Holmes refers to "the curious incident of the dog in the night-time." Watson objects, "But the dog did nothing in the night-time!" and Holmes replies, "That was the curious incident." A dog that *should have barked* because a stranger entered the horse's stall *didn't bark*, and therefore the person entering that stall wasn't a stranger. The absence of a clue became the clue that pointed to a suspect.

This is a truly wonderful device in that the reader is usually going to elide over the missing clue without catching on to its absence until your detective points out that something should have happened that didn't happen. First, however, the writer must establish that the thing that should have happened should have happened. Doyle has several witnesses telling Holmes about the dog's usefulness as a watchdog, and the animal barks at Holmes and Watson when they approach the stall. Even though Holmes doesn't ask point blank whether the dog barked during the night, no one mentions hearing it bark when they recount the incident.

What Is a Clue?

Old-school mystery writers centered their clues in the realm of the physical. We're talking time of death, distances and times and alibis, things left at the scene and things taken from the scene. They knew what a lot of moderns seem not to know: *motive is not a clue.*

Motive is "suggestive" in the words of Sherlock Holmes, but it is not an element of the crime in a court of law. Face it, many innocent people have what someone might see as a motive to kill another person, and if that motive is all they have, no charges will be brought against them.

Clues are:
- Objects found at the scene of the crime
- Fingerprints, fibers, hairs, blood
- Footprints, tire treads
- Bullet holes, stab wounds, poison in the body
- Financial records
- Eyewitness accounts
- Condition of the body
- Location of the body
- Physical evidence pointing to a particular suspect

Not clues but suggestive:
- Lies
- Discrepancies
- Phony alibis (a form of lying, after all)
- Fleeing the scene
- Refusal to answer questions
- Lies of omission, half truths
- Confessions
- Hitherto unrevealed connections between parties

Where Do You Get Your Clues?

Let's go back to the straight-line narrative, the step-by-step account of the murder. Let's divide the straight-line narrative into sections, and see how each section creates its own set of clues. The murderer will create witnesses to her actions somewhere along the line, she will leave traces of herself behind at the scene, she will make mistakes—and it is from these that your clues will emerge.

Preparation for the Crime

Sweet, shy, mousy Wanda wants to kill her Uncle Sebastian before he can disinherit her. To this end, she decides to buy poison. Not being stupid, she doesn't go into her own village, but instead makes a long, arduous trip to a place where she isn't known. Even with this precaution, however, there are going to be witnesses who can tell the detective something about this journey.

First, she took buses. Someone on the bus, a driver or another passenger, will be able to recall a woman of about Wanda's age asking about the connecting bus to Market Finsbury. "She was that nervous, me Lord, she kept wringing her hands and all I could think was, you're in trouble, you are," the witness says, and Lord Bright immediately recognizes Wanda's nervous habit of wringing her hands.

Second, she entered a chemist's shop and bought cyanide. In Britain, this meant signing a book so there would be a record of all poison sales. Again, Wanda wasn't dumb enough to sign her real name, but she still left clues.

> Lord Bright took out his pocket magnifying glass and examined the signature. The name "Maud Silver" rang a very faint bell in his mind (he will later remember that Wanda, Winnie, and Waldo once had a governess by that name). Lord Bright studied the swirls and loops and concluded that the signature was that of a woman over thirty-five, for that particular style had been replaced twenty years ago by the Palmer method. The ink was blue-black and the pen nib very fine; Lord Bright smiled as he remembered the grocery list he'd seen in the cook's hand. It was written in just such ink with just such a fine tip. The person who gave orders to the cook was the daughter who lived in the house; it appeared that Wanda had some explaining to do.

Actually, it would be better if Lord Bright didn't realize all of these things at once; he could see the cook's note later on and connect it with the chemist's book. The point is that Wanda left clues to her identity behind even as she tried to conceal that identity. And even if she'd been smart enough to use her brother's thick-nibbed pen instead of her own, something in that handwriting could give her away.

At the Crime Scene

It's a truism in real detective work that every killer takes something away from the crime scene and also leaves something behind. In today's high-tech investigations, what is taken and what is left can be as small as a microscopic flake of skin containing all the DNA the cops will need to nail their killer.

The real crime scene in Uncle Sebastian's murder is not the dining room table at which he ingested the poisoned port, but the study in which the port was kept and where Wanda had to go to put the poison into the decanter.

What did she take from the scene?

She walked across the rug—could she have a minute thread from the rug on her house slippers? Since she adamantly denies having been in the room, how would a thread from a genuine Persian rug—the only Persian rug in the house—get on her slipper?

What did she leave at the scene?

She picked up the glass decanter, took off its top, and poured poison into it. She touched the glass and left fingerprints.

But she wiped those off, of course.

Did she? Did she wipe the decanter itself but forget to wipe the stopper? Did she wipe the glass but fail to realize that she'd rested her hand for a moment on the corner of the desk?

How did she get into a locked room in the first place? We decided in the straight-line narrative that she diverted the housekeeper's attention by having her boyfriend pose as a salesman. That gives us a witness; when the housekeeper sees a photograph of Hosmer Angel she recognizes the "salesman" even though he was wearing a phony mustache.

Perhaps there's a second witness as well. The gardener might have caught a glimpse of her through the window while she was in the study (she made a big mistake wearing that orange sweater).

The Body Itself

Since this is a poison case, that's the main clue the body can give us. Uncle Sebastian didn't die, as his relatives might first have assumed, from a stroke. Their second assumption—that eating oysters in a month that didn't end with *R* polished him off—is also disproved by the presence of cyanide in his body.

It is the cyanide that leads Lord Bright to make the rounds of chemists' shops within a fifty-mile radius.

Other bodies give us even more scope for clues, not all of them directly related to the cause of death. A death by drowning yields bruises that didn't come from immersion in water, a stabbing victim has traces of narcotics in his system, a body killed by a gunshot also shows signs of defensive wounds on her hands. Perhaps the killer did both—or perhaps a second perpetrator caused a second set of injuries. Either way, the detective has a line of inquiry to pursue, which will lead either to the killer or to a fine fat red herring.

Each particular means of death yields its own special clues. Gunshots give us bullets or fragments inside the body; ballistics can tell us the make of gun. Powder burns determine how close the shooter was to his victim. Knives have edges—and those edges are straight or serrated, single- or double-edged, belong to a short or long blade.

Your detective, whether police or private, needs to make use of forensic clues. In *Chinatown*, the discovery that a man who supposedly drowned in a freshwater reservoir had salt water in his lungs leads Jake Gittes to the truth that the man really died in a pond filled with salt water.

Acts of Concealment

Wanda worked hard to conceal her motive, her access to the means of death, and her opportunity to commit the murder. But she didn't stop there: she decided to go one step further and implicate her family in the crime, planting evidence that will incriminate her brother, sister, and mother. For example:

When Wanda slips into the study to poison the port, she takes with her a diamond comb belonging to her sister, Winnie. She drops this comb under her uncle's desk, where it will be found by Inspector Dim, who will immediately accuse the money-hungry Winnie of the crime.

But how did she get that comb in the first place? Did she steal it from her sister's bedroom, and, if so, what else did she take and what did she leave behind? Winnie's room becomes a secondary crime scene, and another opportunity for clue-creation.

She took strands of hair. Winnie's comb had a few stray strands remaining in it, and they came along with the comb. Then Wanda put the comb in the pocket of her tweed skirt. When she pulled the comb out to plant it in the study, a stray hair stayed behind. When Lord Bright gets the gardener's evidence that he saw something orange in the study on the afternoon the port was poisoned, his lordship remembers that Wanda wore her orange jumper (that's British for sweater) with a brown tweed skirt. He checks the pocket of that skirt and finds a peroxided blond hair that could only belong to sister Winnie. He deduces that Wanda stole and planted Winnie's comb.

Now take each of the other suspects and play the same game. Everywhere Wanda went and everything Wanda did to a) commit the crime, and b) cover up the crime by implicating others, become a fertile source of clues.

Clues in the Private Eye Novel

The classic whodunit involves murder within a small circle of suspects. The private eye novel, set in "the great wrong place" that is the city, *theoretically* involves a much larger world in which anyone could have committed the crime. If we were dealing in reality, any citizen of Los Angeles could have killed our victim, for any reason or for no reason at all. It's Chinatown, Jake.

But the private eye novel isn't any more real than the country-house cozy. It's an "existential romance," a pseudo-realistic vision that is considerably more stylized than truly authentic. We readers love the illusion of looking upon naked, gritty urban reality while at the same time we are comforted by the presence of a detective who carries a banner of honor into the moral swamp.

The private eye combs the city for clues and suspects, and often hops a plane to New Jersey or drives to Vegas to track down a lead. This helps us believe the notion that we are reading realism, that the murderer could be anybody anywhere. Yet when the murderer is revealed, he'd better not be a faceless hit man from Detroit or a passing wino. He'd better be someone we've met or at least heard about before. He'd better be someone we suspected or should have suspected all along and not a bolt from the blue.

Instead of occupying more or less the same space at the same time, as in the traditional mystery, the private eye story gives us suspects who seem on the surface to have nothing in common. The private eye travels to the lowest depths of the city and then interrogates a suspect in a six-million-dollar beach house. One of the pleasures of this kind of mystery is figuring out what connects the two characters in the disparate settings. The connections are usually subterranean, running deep underneath the public lives of the characters like underground sewers.

The private eye picks up few threads and does little apparent ratiocination. Instead, she's more likely to do hands-on investigative research in the public records office, hunting for old birth and death certificates, articles of incorporation, real estate records—tangible proof of links between characters in the distant or not-so-distant past.

The straight-line narrative is still useful here, but less so than in the traditional mystery, since the murder appears so much more open-ended. There are no locked rooms, few phony alibis, and the "frame" is likely to consist of little more than a phone call to some poor sap who gets caught standing over the body bleating, "But he was already dead when I got here!"

Clues in the Police Procedural

If the private eye novel is less realistic than it appears to be, the police procedural is equally fantastic when compared to the truth about police investigations. For one thing, even the 87th Precinct novels fail to capture the fragmented quality of real life detective work. One detective doesn't devote his entire workday to a single case, and one detective doesn't work alone.

Not only do cops come in pairs or teams, but the investigative functions are divided among crime scene technicians, coroners, fingerprint experts, blood and body fluid experts, forensic entomologists, document experts—a whole host of scientists whose job is to back up the street investigators. The cops themselves question witnesses; that's their primary contribution to the case. Their interrogations are backed up by facts discovered through science, but they themselves don't do the science.

In the real world, the killer really could be anyone. There's no playing fair in real life, no small circle of suspects or even subterranean links among a small group. All these *may* be present, but in reality, the killer just might be a passing stranger or a serial killer with no rational motive. As mystery readers, if we want that much reality, we'll read true crime. Fictional police procedurals give the reader the illusion of following real cops through real cases, but they usually edit reality to fit our preconceptions. As with the other forms of the mystery, we'll be introduced to a set of suspects and a case will be made against each in turn. At the end of the book, one of them will be revealed as the true murderer and the others will have been changed in some way by the fact of the investigation.

Whichever subgenre you choose, you'll need to plant clues for your detective to find, and a step-by-step account of the murder and the cover-up is the best way to develop those clues.

3. Build Me an Arc, I

The Structure of the Mystery Novel

EVERY NOVEL needs some kind of structure. At the very least, a story starts at the beginning, moves through the middle, and ends at the end.

What kinds of things need to happen in the beginning of the mystery novel, in the middle, and at the end in order to give the reader the satisfaction she wanted when she bought the book?

Arc One: The Beginning (The Setup)

The beginning of any novel is the setup, in which the reader is introduced to the characters, the setting, and the situation that will dominate the rest of the story. Many cozy whodunits begin by introducing the suspects *before* the murder is committed. We meet an eminently murderable citizen, and we see that citizen interacting with a number of people he aggravates to the point at which they mutter something about how "he's gonna get himself killed one of these days."

That's the way Carolyn G. Hart's *The Christie Caper* begins. We spend Arc One wondering what new outrage cozy-hating mystery critic Neil Bledsoe will perpetrate next, and how long it will take someone to succeed in killing him. Several attempts are made, but our intrepid sleuth Annie Laurence Darling, owner of a mystery bookstore, reminds us of the advice given by Miss Jane Marple: "Nothing is ever quite what it appears to be on the surface."

Diane Mott Davidson's *Catering to Nobody* opens with a wake marking the passing by suicide (or was it?) of a teacher. At the wake one of the

The Four-Arc System for Organizing Your Novel

The beauty of this plan is that you can use it as a blueprint before you've written a single word, or you can plunge ahead at full speed and then reorganize your material accordingly.

Think of your novel as having four parts, roughly 70–80 manuscript pages each in length (based on a total length of 300 pages; longer books have longer arcs). Each of these parts has a distinct purpose in telling your story.

Ten-Minute Hook
An opening scene or chapter that is self-contained and grabs the reader in some way, by either showing a "day in the life" of the character whose life is about to be turned upside down, or giving a mini-preview of things to come.

Arc One
- Set up the conflict or problem, introduce main character and opponent or mystery
- Establish character's inner need, which s/he may or may not be aware of
- Start the subplot rolling—either main character's or a secondary character's or both
- *No flashbacks allowed*—tell reader *only* what he must know *now*
- Make the contract with the reader through tone and style
- Use a catalyst if appropriate to get story started and keep things moving

End Arc One at a crisis: the first turning point scene changes everything and sends the main character in pursuit of a new goal. A decision leads to a beginning level of commitment.

Arc Two
- Here come the flashbacks—but *only* to illuminate the present
- Main character is tested, trained, given tasks, tries and fails to reach goal
- One step forward, two steps back
- Each gain leads to a (greater) loss in the end
- Subplots deepen, also move toward their crunch points
- Discrepancy between character's wants and needs grows larger
- Establish deadline or ticking bomb, beyond which all will be lost

End Arc Two at a crisis: the Midpoint scene may involve hitting bottom, being convinced there is no hope of success. Or the main character may move from reactive to proactive, from committed to fanatical, from objective to emotionally involved, from wrong goal to right goal. A line may well be crossed. Return to the status quo is now impossible. The character can only go forward, come what may.

Arc Three

- Pace increases considerably; chapters and sentences are shorter
- All threads begin coming together; all subplots will be resolved by end
- Ticking time bomb or other deadline becomes compelling
- Build toward climax with ever-increasing conflicts and consequences
- Character's desire to reach goal increases exponentially
- Disconnect between character's need and want becomes clear even to him
- Character tested and trained for the ultimate confrontation

End with Arc Three crisis, the second turning point, in which the character is forced to make a crucial decision. This can be a low point (if character hasn't already hit bottom), or it can be a recognition that nothing short of a life-or-death confrontation will solve problem.

Arc Four

- The showdown at last—Good faces Evil, and only one will survive
- All the stakes are bet on a single hand; nothing is held back
- Give the ending its full value—give the reader what you promised in Arc One
- Use all the elements you set up in the earlier arcs for maximum payoff now
- Make sure character undergoes both external and internal transformation
- Show an outer manifestation of internal change—character does something in a way he or she couldn't have done at the beginning of the story
- Make sure subplot resolution either supports or contrasts with main plot resolution for maximum thematic impact
- If at all possible, take characters full circle in some way, with a setting or situation that repeats and echoes the beginning

guests has a stomach attack and the cops suspect poison. Caterer Goldy Bear must delve into the poisoning in order to save her business, but she eventually comes to believe that the "suicide" was murder.

Both Annie Laurence Darling and Goldy Bear make explicit decisions to investigate the crimes early in the story. That decision to "take the case" is the close of the first act, the place at which the detection begins.

It's also known as Plot Point One, or the end of Arc One in the Four-Arc System. The murder itself is *not*, as some might think, the turning point—after all, people are murdered every day and their friends don't step in to solve the crime. Murder itself is not the essence of the detective story. It is the amateur detective's decision to "take the case" and solve the crime that makes the book a classic mystery.

The police officer is different. It is, after all, his job to solve murders, so "taking the case" is assumed. Many police procedurals begin, not with a lineup of suspects, but with the dead body on the floor. This means one of the author's main tasks in the first arc will be to introduce the reader to the victim—a task the cozy writer did while the victim was alive.

When does Arc One reach Plot Point One if the body is already on the floor in the first chapter? One answer: when the case becomes personal, takes on meanings that make it more than just another case. This can involve the cop's personal emotions, or his relationship within his community, or larger political and social implications. Being warned to lay off a major suspect because he's connected makes the case personal for some police officers. The important thing is that something near the end of the introductory material changes the nature of the case or the nature of the cop's relationship to the case, forcing a different attitude and approach in Arc Two.

Private eye novels have their own unique variation on this structure. Usually, the P.I. "takes the case" in chapter one—but the case she takes is seldom a murder. She is asked to find a lost daughter or tail an unfaithful husband or check out a bogus insurance claim. The routine case turns into a murder case at the end of Arc One, thus raising the stakes and changing the detective's focus. Instead of (or in addition to) a murder, the P.I. may find that her client has lied to her, or be warned off the case by cops or people with power in the community. In any case, the routine matter she started with has turned deadly, and that will alter her behavior and focus in Arc Two.

Arc Two: The Big Bad Middle _____

Writing the middle of a novel is a lot like driving through Texas. You think it's never going to end, and all the scenery looks the same.

So what breaks the monotony? How can you keep the tension high as your detective essentially plods through the detail-oriented work of criminal investigation?

In a detective story, the detective detects. In case you think that's too obvious to need mentioning, take notes when you read your next mystery and ask yourself whether its amateur sleuth is really detecting or over-hearing things, listening to confessions, making wild speculations and wilder connections—in short, is that detective detecting or just getting lucky? The true detective story involves deductive reasoning, the use of logic, and speculation based on concrete evidence.

When the detective detects is in the middle of the book. How the detective detects depends in part on the subgenre we're in. The amateur detective and the private eye are limited by the fact that nobody *has* to talk to him. The cop can compel answers, but she also inspires fear, and fear leads to lawyers, who will definitely call a halt to questioning.

Detecting: The Q&A

Questions and answers are a major source of information for the detective. This is dangerous for the writer because it leads to a lot of talking heads scenes, which can become boring and repetitive. How to spark up those scenes?

- Choose an interesting setting. This might mean tracking the witness down at work—and making that work as fascinating as possible. If you take the Q&A into the witness's house, give us a house to remember.

- Don't let all the witnesses roll over. Someone, somewhere, sometime should refuse to talk to the detective. This at least breaks the rhythm of one "confession" after another.

- It wouldn't hurt if someone threw a punch instead of answering questions. The workplace setting can be of great help with this, particularly if it's a place with dangerous objects all around.

- People have been known to lie. Maybe they could lie to your detective. The downside is that he probably won't know it's a lie until later.

- Evasion is good, too. What if our witness is amazingly forthcoming about one aspect of the case and then clams up as soon as a certain name is mentioned? That adds interest to the scene without resorting to violence.

- Even if you have to use the talking-heads-over-coffee setup for your Q&A, there are other ways to put spin on the ball, most notably by making the witnesses very interesting characters with a lot of quirks and zippy dialogue. Humor helps. Always.

Ever watch *Law and Order*? You should; every mystery writer can learn from that first half hour of police work as the detectives track down the perpetrator of the crime we saw in the first two minutes of the show.

What are the lessons of *Law and Order* (which owes a great deal to its predecessor, *Dragnet*) when it comes to presenting zippy Q&A?

First, the cops waste no time getting to where they're going. We start the scene at the witness's home or workplace without wasting time showing the cops making the trip.

Unless they're doing a quick discussion of exactly what it is they want to learn from this witness, in which case the point of the scene isn't to show them eating a hot dog while strolling down Seventh Avenue, it's to let the viewer know which piece of evidence this witness will or will not deliver into their hands and to remind us where that piece fits into their theory of the case.

Once they're in place, the detectives get right to the point. "Where were you on the night of the twelfth?" The answer given by Witness A takes them directly to Witness B, Witness B puts them on to Witness C—sometimes directly, sometimes indirectly—and quite often Witness D sends them back to A now that they realize A was concealing something.

The show's writers make a point of varying ages, races, genders, and economic backgrounds. The detectives go into the penthouses of the rich and famous and then to the cardboard box that's home to another witness. One witness has a Wall Street office with a view to die for, the next works on the loading dock. The rich threaten the cops with lawyers; the poor just threaten. The variation, and the deliberate insertion of the cops into alien territory, adds interest to what are essentially talking heads scenes.

Because they're cops, they have the option of "squeezing" witnesses who don't want to talk. Sometimes this leads to one witness ratting out another, or it may allow the cops to move up the chain of command in a criminal enterprise.

And it all happens so fast. That's the real magic of that first half-hour. We saw a crime in progress and in twenty-two minutes the detectives have a suspect arrested and ready for trial. They've spun and discarded four or five theories of the case, interrogated eight to ten witnesses, followed three or four distinct lines of inquiry, and they even had time for snappy banter, not to mention that hot dog.

Detecting: Physical Evidence

Questioning suspects and witnesses isn't the only way to get information. In the Golden Age, the Great Detective got down on all fours and checked the carpet for loose threads, mainly because the police didn't understand or respect scientific evidence, but today the police know all there is to know about forensics and they're the ones on their knees. So if your detective is a police officer, you can use all the forensic tricks you want to nail your suspect. Just make sure those details are interesting to the reader.

If your detective is an amateur or a private eye, you have a problem. The crime scene technicians and homicide detectives aren't going to let your sleuth anywhere near the sources of physical evidence. Only if your detective finds the body before the cops are called is there a chance of seeing that evidence firsthand.

Not that seeing it will be enough. The scientific knowledge and technology needed to match hairs and threads, blood and saliva, just don't belong to ordinary people. You need science, and the cops have all the science.

Your detective, however, might borrow a little science by finding out what the cops know. This is one reason why so many female amateur detectives have cop boyfriends—it's one way to be certain that such details as time of death are revealed to the detective. Some facts will be reported in the newspapers, and the private detective often has sources on the papers who turn over what the newspaper withholds.

Private eyes are expected to have people they can turn to for information outside of official channels. Amateurs, on the other hand, are ordinary people, and the writer who gives them unlimited access to inside information is in danger of losing credibility.

If you can't get your detective to the body, how can your detective make use of physical evidence?

How about the victim's house, car, office, gym locker? Your detective just might have a chance at beating the cops to one of these places, and all of them present interesting opportunities for clue finding. Messages on answering machines, computer disks, letters, diaries, notes, prescription drugs in medicine cabinets, lipstick on the collar, whips in the closet, stacks of money under the floorboards, diamonds in the ice cubes, narcotics in the briefcase, blood on the fender, a dead body in the bathtub—the possibilities are endless.

In *Catering to Nobody*, Goldy Bear has a free hand in her investigation of the supposed suicide because the police discount the idea that it was murder. Through a series of ruses and assertive moves, she gains access to the dead woman's house, her car, her gym locker, and her pharmacy records. She also listens to small-town rumor and finds evidence in her son's desk drawer at school. She collects enough evidence to force the police to consider that the woman was murdered.

To reveal or not to reveal, that is the question. The unofficial detective, whether P.I. or amateur, always confronts the issue of whether, when, and how to let the police in on what he's discovered. Note that I'm not talking about sharing speculations with the cops but behaving like a good citizen and letting the police know that there's vital evidence over here.

P.I.s like to grab that diary and run. They like to make anonymous phone calls about the body in the tub, then hotfoot it to Fresno to talk to a witness before the cops find out that witness even exists. Working outside the law, sometimes deliberately getting in the way of the law, is part of the code.

The amateur is different. We're less likely to go along with flat-out obstruction of justice if the detective is a normal person. We have a bias toward letting the official police do their jobs—so long as those official police are seen as good guys.

So one way to justify withholding evidence is to present the reader with cops who are either on the take or criminally stupid. Perhaps they've arrested The Wrong Man, in which case they not only won't be interested in evidence pointing to someone else, they'll deny that the evidence is evidence at all. If they're on the take, not only will they refuse to believe the evidence; they might even destroy it to preserve their wrongheaded theory. So why bother giving it to them?

Detecting: Reasoning

The detective detects. Part of the detecting is the Q&A, another part is collecting physical evidence, and a third, very important, part is thinking about what she's learned. Thinking is a vital middlebook act in mysteries.

But thinking isn't visual or dramatic or, let's face it, inherently interesting. So how does the mystery writer make it worth reading?

Add a second character, a sidekick, a person with whom the detective can shoot the breeze, air his opinions, bounce ideas back and forth—in short, a Watson.

But won't scenes where the detective and his Watson mull things over become just another talking heads scene? What are some ways to add spice to those inevitable "It could have been George; but what about Martha, she hated him, too" scenes?

- Could the detective and the sidekick argue about who's right? Archie Goodwin often disapproves of Nero Wolfe's suspicions, and we enjoy their byplay more because Archie's not a fawning pushover.

- Some sidekicks do a bit of detecting of their own. When Anne Perry's Inspector Pitt sits down to dinner with his wife, Charlotte, they both have information to share because they've both interrogated different people during the day. (One reason why they investigate in different spheres: the mores of the Victorian Age. Pitt is the official police detective, but the secret, shared world of women is one he cannot penetrate. He needs the information Charlotte can discover by being a woman and a member of the upper class. The key to detective duos is giving each a separate skill or sphere.)

- The Golden Age detectives act out the crime, reconstructing the walk to the train station in order to determine if the witness lied about how long it took. Adding physicality to a whodunit scene is always a good idea.

- Try not to put all the speculation in one big scene. Let the detective rethink his position every time he learns something new. This is what the *Law and Order* cops do as they race from place to place, and it gives context to the individual interrogations.

- Other Golden Age ideas that shouldn't be abandoned are the written timeline, the hand-drawn map, the diagram of the room showing where everyone was standing at the time of the murder; in short, the raw data that feeds the detective's speculation. Let the reader see these and she will engage more fully in the act of detecting.

Annie and Max, the detective duo in *The Christie Caper*, do their thinking the old-fashioned way—and Dame Agatha would surely have approved. They create homemade maps of the attempted murder scenes, lists of suspects and where they were at the relevant times, and have discussions where they compare notes and speculate on the murder.

One important aspect of the Thinking sections of the mystery is that anything the clever reader could come up with by way of explanation must also be considered by the detective if she is to live up to the name. *Catering to Nobody* introduces Goldy Bear and her preteen son, Arch, a troubled boy with a penchant for Dungeons and Dragons. When Goldy learns that her son hated his grandfather, the victim of the attempted poisoning, she allows herself a moment to wonder if her own child could have slipped the poison into the man's coffee. She discards the theory, but at least the reader realizes she's aware of the possibility. Had Davidson ignored Arch as a suspect, the reader would have felt superior to Goldy instead of those two steps behind that the writer wanted us to be.

Midpoint

Arc Two ends—where? What marks the Midpoint of the book, the beginning of Arc Three?

Something should. The danger is that the middle continues with detection, with Q&A, with speculation, all of the same variety and intensity as in Arc Two. This is what reviewers mean when they say a book sags in the middle.

So what changes?

A second body is always good—*but only if the body is more than a body.*

Only if the second body changes everything does it really make a good Midpoint.

How does it change everything? In *The Christie Caper*, the body changes everything because, contrary to the reader's expectation, *it isn't Bledsoe's*. The man we love to hate, the man whose murder we've been expecting since page one is still alive and breathing and someone else, someone we gave no thought to, is lying dead instead.

The second body, or in this case, the first successful murder attempt, changes everything by knocking the detective's theory into a cocked hat. For this to happen, the detective has to *have* a theory in the first place, and he has to be pretty well convinced of it, or knocking it down won't mean much to him. Setting up the impact of the second body, then, requires that our detective have done a fair amount of work in Arc Two, that he's eliminated some suspects and zeroed in on others, and that he's got what he thinks is a clear picture of events. He's narrowed the suspects to one or two, he's proved certain alibis and uncovered certain motives. He's exposed lies and revealed inconsistencies, and he's feeling pretty good about himself.

The impact of Body Two is that the one or two suspects he's focused on *couldn't possibly have committed this crime.* One good reason for being unable to kill Victim Two is that the prime suspect *is* Victim Two. Another good reason is that Victim Two apparently has no connection to Victim One, and yet they were both clearly killed by the same person. Or Victim Two is a person no one has an obvious motive to kill, yet there he is, dead, and his death is a reproach to the detective for not having solved the crime.

Emotional resonance can be added by having the second body be that of a person we actually liked. This gives the detective even more motivation to get to the truth of the matter.

Does the Midpoint event that changes everything have to be a second body?

No, but it helps. The essence of the Midpoint is that shift from one investigational direction to another. Being warned off the case might change everything if the warning comes from someone who shouldn't have a deep interest in the original murder. Violence or danger to the detective in and of itself is *not* really a Midpoint event if all it does is add more pressure without changing the direction of the investigation. The essence of Midpoint—of the shift from Arc Two to Arc Three—is that the detective must double back, must rethink, must re-examine everything he's already done.

And if the writer has done his job, the detective is not only back to square one, but also *worse off* than he was when he began the investigation. For one thing, he probably knows now that at least one of the witnesses he questioned was lying. He may even know which one—the one lying on a slab at the morgue. How will he get the information that witness had now?

Arc Three: Waist-Deep in the Big Muddy

Law and Order moves to the lawyers for its Arc Three, and what usually happens is that a case that seemed straightforward suddenly develops more holes than the *Titanic*. A confession is thrown out, physical evidence is suppressed, and the person we thought was guilty turns out to be covering up for the real killer.

Back to Square One—or is it? Isn't it "back a couple of steps *before* Square One"? Because now the cops need evidence independent of that smoking gun the judge suppressed. The best evidence they had is gone; the witnesses they already talked to aren't likely to change their stories without a lot more pressure being put on them. That's the essence of Arc Three in the mystery: to make the solving of this crime seem a complete impossibility thanks to the Midpoint development. In *Law and Order*, because of its unique structure, that development is usually a legal twist. In an ordinary mystery, it has to be something else.

Arc Three often involves revisiting the witnesses already questioned in Arc Two. But we question them now with a greater sense of intensity and we know things we didn't know in Arc Two. We perhaps apply more pressure to get the answers we want—if there's a danger of the detective crossing the line to force people to talk, now is when he will cross that line. The straight-arrow cop becomes Dirty Harry and the Dirty Harry cop goes ballistic.

Violence escalates. The murderer uses violence to silence witnesses and to intimidate the detective. Our police detective goes too far in his interrogation of someone with connections and is taken off the case. The private eye gets fired by his own client, who now seems eager to forget the whole thing.

Subplots coalesce with the main plot. Arc Three is where the detective figures out what astute readers have suspected all along: those two seemingly unrelated cases he's been working on are connected in some subtle, subterranean way. This happens in *Catering to Nobody*, and the realization of that connection changes everything, and forces Goldy to re-examine all she's learned and deduced from the beginning.

That's part of the funhouse effect. What looked "normal" in the mirror is really a distorted picture of reality. What seemed authentic was bogus; what seemed a lie was only the truth in a thin disguise. Now that we know the entire truth, everything that went before becomes suddenly clear. When Jake Gittes finally understands Evelyn Cross Mulwray's anguished cry, "She's my sister *and* my daughter!" it all falls into place. What seemed murky is now both clear and terrible, worse than anything Gittes imagined, and yet completely believable in terms of what we know about Noah Cross.

Challenge to the Reader

Ellery Queen, one of the great detective writers of the Golden Age, introduced a device called Challenge to the Reader. When Ellery the detective character finally figured out who did it, he'd shout, "Eureka!" and jump out of his chair, ready to confront the criminal. End of chapter, and, by the way, Plot Point Two.

Queen didn't start the next chapter on the next page. Instead, he inserted a one-page Challenge to the Reader, which said that the reader was privy to all the clues Ellery had unearthed, and invited the reader to put the book down, rethink everything he'd read, and match wits with the Great Detective.

In other words, the Challenge gave readers a chance to pause and think before turning the page and finding out the solution.

Did it work? Did millions of readers—and Queen was a best-seller in his day—actually put down their books and stare at the ceiling, hoping for enlightenment? Did they jot down clues, make little maps of the crime scene, flip the pages back to reread certain sections of the book before arriving at their well-reasoned conclusions?

I have no idea.

What I do know is that if you catch an episode of *Murder, She Wrote*, there will be a scene in which Jessica Fletcher jumps from her chair, eyes wide, says, "I know who killed him!" and races off to confront the killer.

Cut to commercial.

That's the Challenge to the Reader. Not only are you supposed to run to the refrigerator or the bathroom, you're supposed to think for a minute about whom you suspect and whom you think Jessica suspects and why. It's the writer's way of playing fair with the reader, of saying, "You have the clues; now solve the crime."

Both Carolyn G. Hart and Diane Mott Davidson, whose books are firmly in the classic whodunit tradition, use Challenge to the Reader. In *Catering*, Goldy realizes who the killer is and reveals her suspicion to the investigating police officer on p. 279. She doesn't share her conclusion or the reasoning supporting it with the reader until p. 284 when she gathers all the suspects together. *The Christie Caper* follows a similar pattern. Annie reviews her notes on p. 293 and sees a discrepancy. "A false note," she muses. "If that was false, what else might be false?" She has her solution on p. 294, but doesn't reveal it until p. 299, giving the reader a chance to play the game and come up with the false note and its meaning.

Once you've introduced your Challenge to the Reader, it's your job to lay your solution to the crime before your reader. The ending is so important to the reader's experience that it gets an entire chapter of its own.

4. Endings are Hard, I

Satisfying the Mystery Reader

ENDINGS ARE HARD. Once upon a time, in the Golden Age, it was enough for the Great Detective to *know*. Ellery Queen gathered all the suspects together in the drawing room and proceeded to spend seven or eight closely reasoned pages expounding his theory on who had done what and why, clearing up any loose ends along the way. (I once saw a *New Yorker* cartoon that parodied this scene by showing the Great Detective as a parrot sitting on a perch with all the suspects in front of him.) Occasionally the disgruntled suspect pulled a gun and made a break for it, only to be subdued by the burly Sergeant Velie, but action wasn't the essence of the scene.

Across the water, Lord Peter Wimsey conducted his expository scene in a tête-à-tête with the murderer, then quietly withdrew to permit the killer an "honorable way out": pistols for one in the library. Sometimes Dr. Gideon Fell decided the killer was a better man than his victim and played judge and jury, leaving the official solution of the crime to the police he knew were incompetent to solve it.

Knowing was enough. Justice in terms of courtrooms and jury verdicts was decidedly secondary.

No one expected the Great Detective to wrestle the killer to the ground and pluck the loaded gun from his hand, or to plug the killer between the eyes.

But we *do* tend to expect action endings from Kinsey Millhone and Matt Scudder. We won't be satisfied with V.I. Warshawski calling the cops and going home for a hot bath; we want her on the scene dodging bullets. When Hercule Poirot confronted twelve killers at once, we had no reason to fear for his safety; that wasn't how the game was played. But put Elvis Cole on the *Orient Express*, and we won't be happy if all he does is talk. In the Second Golden Age, we want our detectives to go *mano-a-mano* with the killer; knowing is no longer enough.

The result is that the scene in which the detective confronts the killer has become as clichéd, as predictable, as the old-fashioned drawing-room gathering. We can see it coming a mile away; the amateur detective who grows herbs for a living and who ought to turn the matter over to the police is heading for an abandoned building to meet the man she's sure is the killer. He's armed; she's not—and if you have any doubt about which of them is going to prevail, you haven't done enough reading. She, after all, is on her fourth book of a series.

So one question to ask yourself when you're about to confront your own ending: does the detective absolutely have to go one-on-one with the killer?

The Non-Action Ending

No. It is still possible to write a satisfying mystery novel without a physical set-to between detective and killer. Take a look at Margaret Maron's *Southern Discomfort*. Instead of confrontation, we have a horrified realization that tragic misunderstandings led to murder. We have a ripple effect that touches everyone connected with the mystery and is more powerful by far than a simpler, more violent, ending could have been. Similarly, Sue Dunlap in *Rogue Wave* gives us emotional resonance and poetic justice without resorting to the traditional wresting-the-gun-from-the-killer's-hand scene.

Sometimes the revelation isn't so much a matter of who the criminal is as why he did what he did. Unusual motives that ring true in terms of character can be found in Robert Barnard's *Fête Fatale* and Reginald Hill's *Ruling Passions*. The story behind the murder is a major reason why Minette Walters, P.D. James, Elizabeth George, and Val McDermid sell so many books.

Hill, a grandmaster of the genre, uses other interesting devices to vary the predictability of the whodunit ending: in *Pictures of Perfection*, he opens the book with a gunman shooting at a crowd of people at a garden fête (another fatal fête!). He then backs the story up so that it concludes with the same shooting, and only then do we find out not only what was behind the shooting but also who lives and who dies. In a similar vein, Hill's *Bones and Silence* creates ongoing suspense throughout the mystery by showing letters to a police officer from an unidentified suicidal woman. Only at the end do we find out who this woman is and whether or not she succeeds in her tragic effort to take her own life.

The Two-Layered Ending

Another traditional twist is the two-layered ending (for example, *The Tragedy of Y* by Ellery Queen). The detective apparently solves the crime, produces evidence of one actor behind the events—only to discover a second layer, a second culprit, another mind behind the murders. This ending is used to great effect in *If Ever I Return, Pretty Peggy-O* by Sharyn McCrumb, and *Time Expired* by Sue Dunlap. It satisfies our mystery-lover's longing for a complex puzzle while deepening emotional resonance through the connections between the two minds.

Two-layered endings don't always mean two murderous minds at work. One of Ellery Queen's hallmarks was the "public consumption" solution, delivered with full flourishes in front of the police, and the "just-between-us" solution given to the victim's family. We readers believed the first one, and then were told we'd had the wool pulled over our eyes and now we'd learn the truly true truth.

On a couple of memorable occasions, Ellery even slipped in a third solution.

Why Endings Fail

What kinds of mystery endings disappoint readers?

- The "eenie, meenie, miney, moe" ending in which the murderer could have been any one of the suspects and seems to have been chosen at random for the final "honor" of being the truly guilty party. The revelation of the true killer should give the reader a jolt of recognition: yes, this is right, it all becomes clear to me now. The reader wants a sense of inevitability about the killer's identity. It had to be X; it could only have been X.

- The emotionally unsatisfying ending. A killer has been unmasked but true justice hasn't been done. This is okay in a hard-boiled detective tale whose premise is that justice is impossible, but if we're in cozyland where stability and order are supposed to be restored by the detective's solution to the crime, we won't be happy without some justice. By the same token, dry, arid exposition won't do the trick; we need some emotional resonance to our endings to be fully satisfied today.

- Failing to tie up all the loose ends. It is the detective's job not just to solve the murder but to unravel all the threads, explain everything that needs explaining, rip the masks off the phonies, expose all the lies, cut through all the disguises, tell all the secrets. Smart modern writers unravel a few of these lesser knots along the way, saving the big one, the murder, for the end. But all needs to be explained eventually; you don't want the reader wondering who left the upstairs bedroom window open or why the headmaster lied about playing golf.

- Ambiguity. Mystery readers want certainty in an uncertain world. We don't mind existentialist angst and nihilistic dystopias in our hard-boiled reads, but even those have a certain clarity about them. What we hate is not knowing what really happened. Some top-selling psychological mysteries leave us unclear as to the final identity of the killer and suggest a kind of "group guilt" that ultimately turns off hard-core mystery readers.

- The killer just wasn't important enough throughout the story. He's not chosen at random exactly, but he was sufficiently obscure that the reader scratches her head and says, "Him? I can barely remember him" when he's declared the murderer.

- The author gave us a tricky setup with multiple complications throughout the big bad middle and now the solution is as simplistic as a child's drawing. The payoff doesn't pay off.

- "God in the killer's lap" solutions that depend upon the killer having a lot of good luck all along the way. Coincidence piles upon coincidence until any shred of believability is lost.

- The detective fails to detect. The killer reveals herself to the sleuth instead of the other way around. Sheer dumb luck catapults the so-called detective into a leap of logic that just happens to be true.

- Sudden violence takes the place of logical reasoning and honest investigation. Less jarring in a private eye novel, this can be off-putting if the book has heretofore been a mild cozy and now we're hip-deep in blood.

The Action Ending

If you choose confrontation, accept the fact that it will come as a surprise only to those readers who are entering the world of mystery for the first time. The confrontation scene is a set piece by now, although it still needs to be set up so that your detective appears brave rather than foolhardy. The truth is, we readers crave the action ending, no matter how many critics carp when V.I. Warshawski heads off to that abandoned factory on Chicago's South Side in the next-to-last chapter, so we're ready to suspend disbelief. We just don't want to suspend our entire grip on reality. We want it to be believable that *this* detective places herself in the position of confronting *this* killer. We even seem willing to swallow yet another killer-tells-all-just-before-plugging-detective-between-the-eyes scene, again flying in the face of critical opinion. Yes, it's ridiculous that the killer sits on the edge of the cliff expounding upon his own guilt instead of plugging the detective squarely between the eyes and heading to Peru, but the fact is, the detective's coming back for the next book in the series and the killer isn't, so we read on, no matter how many times we've read this scene in the past.

How can you set your confrontation scene apart from all the others? Short answer: you can't. But you *can* add to its power by setting it in a very interesting—and, of course, highly dangerous—location. It also helps if your detective goes to the confrontation thinking she's prepared, only to find out otherwise when the time comes. She's armed, but someone takes her gun. She's alerted the police, but they don't respond. She thinks she's confronting a mere witness, but the truth is, he's the killer.

The confrontation section in a modern mystery is a mini-suspense novel. You need to switch gears from the puzzle to the roller-coaster ride, to shelve logic and reason and go straight to visceral emotion. You will want to swing the pendulum between safety and danger, between trust and distrust, in exactly the same way the suspense novelist does. The only difference is that she does it for an entire book; you will do it for two or three chapters.

One of the hallmarks of suspense writing is the slowing down of time to an agonizing pace that emphasizes every minute. If you have a ticking time bomb in the background, now is the time to let it tick as loudly as possible, reminding the reader of exactly how many seconds the detective has left before the worst will happen. Read Mary Higgins Clark's *A Stranger Is Watching*—which involves a real time bomb ticking in the basement of Grand Central Station; a time bomb which will kill not only our heroine but a child—and watch how she shows every one of those seconds ticking away as our heroine extricates herself from her bonds. We feel every tug of the rope that ties her, we see the blood trickling down her arms, we experience her agony of despair as she tries and fails to loosen her bonds.

That's what you want in your confrontation scene. The rest of the book may involve the highest levels of ratiocination since the late, great Ellery, but for the confrontation chapters, go for pure adrenaline. Slow down the filmstrip and milk the situation for every ounce of terror. Let the detective feel every possible emotion from deepest despair to exhilarating hope as she struggles with a killer bent on eliminating her.

What, then, is the difference between a suspense ending and a mystery ending with suspense overtones? Suspense is its own reward; we don't care in a suspense novel if we know from page one who the villain is. In a mystery, we can keep the puzzle going even through the confrontation; it's no less satisfying if the detective is shoved into the autoclave by an unknown killer than if he's already identified the villain as Evil Doctor X. The suspense is just an extra on the menu; the main dish is the whodunit.

The Coda

Linda Barnes closes *Snapshot* with a seder. To this traditional Jewish ceremonial dinner her detective Carlotta Carlyle invites a decidedly untraditional family. Carlotta's friends Gloria and Roz (who wears a pink T-shirt that says "Will work for sex"); Roz's new boyfriend, a mobster named Sam Gianelli, Carlotta's Little Sister Paolina and her Colombian family all sit around the table. Now that the crime has been solved, the unorthodox group that surrounds Carlotta has become even closer and they celebrate that closeness with a ceremonial dinner.

The cozy coda shows that the fabric of society has been rewoven after it was torn by the victim and his killer (according to W.H. Auden, the victim was as much a disrupter as the murderer). We see order restored, peace preserved, sheep safely grazing, ordinary life moving along in its ordinary way without the threat of violent death.

Since mysteries now choose to explore aspects of the detective's personal life, the intensely personal coda has become important. Not only has Jenny Cain solved a murder in *I.O.U.*, she has reconciled in some way with her mentally ill mother. Not only did Matt Scudder face down ruthless killers in *Eight Million Ways to Die*, he also faced his own alcoholism. Some detectives find a meaningful relationship; others end one.

The Meta-Novel

I first heard the term "meta-novel" at a writer's conference in Tulsa, Oklahoma. The idea is that even though each book in a series stands alone, when read collectively they form one big ongoing novel about the main character. Each book represents its own arc: in book one of the series we meet the character and establish a meta-goal that will carry him through further books, in book two that meta-goal is tested, in book three—you get the picture.

It's All One Big Book

Looked at this way, every book about Kinsey Millhone, from *A Is for Alibi* to the latest letter of the alphabet, constitutes one big novel with a lot of different episodes, kind of like a television series. As we read through the series, we learn more about Kinsey and we deepen our connection to her so that even minor conflicts in later books mean something to us because we know her so well and we're aware of exactly what pushes her buttons. When something big happens, such as finding lost family members in *J Is for Judgment*, it resonates because we're fully aware of her orphaned childhood.

I always think of *M*A*S*H* when this topic comes up. Remember the episode that focused on the dreams of the regular cast members? Hot Lips Houlihan, who was always searching for love, dreamed that she was a bride—only her white dress was covered in operating room blood.

Klinger, who longed to return to his home town of Toledo, Ohio, dreamed he was on a train going home—only every place in town he wanted to see was boarded up and closed down. Each dream took each character far inside himself, and each dream was understandable and moving because we had known these characters for so long. The thirty-minute episode could go as deep as it did because it followed several years of character exploration.

The same can be true of series characters whose tests become more meaningful when we've seen them through earlier crises. Nancy Pickard's detective heroine, Jenny Cain, solved mysteries about other people's troubles in the early books. *Dead Crazy* brought us face to face with mental illness, and we learned for the first time that Jenny's mother had a mental problem. Not until *I.O.U.*, the seventh book in the series, did Jenny directly confront that past issue, and by that time, we'd seen her grappling with ever-darker social problems. In a sense, the first book in the series *(Generous Death)*, which introduced us to Jenny and her world, was Arc One of the meta-novel. All the six books leading up to *I.O.U.* constituted Arcs Two and Three, in that Jenny honed the investigative and emotional tools she would need to excavate the truth of her mother's life and death. Had Pickard even been able to write *I.O.U.* as the second book in the series, it wouldn't have had nearly the impact upon the reader that it did as book seven because we weren't as invested in Jenny early on.

Multiple Protagonists and the Meta-Novel

Elizabeth George uses five main characters as protagonists, which would be far too many for the reader to handle if she didn't allow some to shine in the foreground and the others to recede into the background of each book. For example, in *A Traitor to Memory*, Lynley and Havers are in the forefront, while Helen and St. James are used sparingly. Other books center on St. James and Helen, with Lynley and Havers as lesser characters, and *Deception on His Mind* takes Havers away from London into an adventure all her own.

S. J. Rozan alternates between her two protagonists, Bill Smith and Lydia Chin. The first book in the series, *China Trade*, was told in Lydia's first-person viewpoint. The second, *Concourse*, used Bill as its protagonist and told the story in third person. This device allows us to see the meta-arc of their developing relationship through two different pairs of eyes.

Reginald Hill gave Sgt. Wield a personal subplot and one of the pleasures of his Dalziel–Pascoe series has been the evolution of the stoic sergeant from walled-off character with a deep secret to a warmer, more open human being. Carole Nelson Douglas says of her Midnight Louie series that it will ultimately consist of twenty-seven books with over-arching story arcs of nine books each. Earlene Fowler's quilt series often brings characters from previous books back into detective Benni Harper's life, as does Abigail Padgett's Bo Bradley series.

Starting a mystery series means thinking beyond book one. It means creating characters compelling enough to pull readers along through many adventures and rich enough to deserve a loyal following.

Part 2:
The Roller Coaster
of Suspense

5. Buckle Up for the Ride

What Is a Suspense Novel?

WE LOVE to be scared, whether it's on a thrill ride or at a scary movie. Suspense novels add a human dimension to the basic excitement of being scared on purpose in a controlled environment. When we read a book by Mary Higgins Clark, Tom Clancy, or John Grisham we identify with the main character, whose life is thrown into turmoil by forces beyond his control, and we experience all the emotions that character feels, whether good or bad. We're afraid when he's afraid; we're confident when he's confident. We go along for the ride, secure in the knowledge that when the ride is over we'll be back on level ground, exhilarated and safe.

The Roller-Coaster Effect

It doesn't matter whether you love, hate, or fear them: you know what it means to ride a roller coaster. Your heart pounds, your palms sweat, your body tenses and then relaxes, your mouth opens and screams come out. You fear for your life one second, then laugh with delight the next as you remind yourself it's only a ride. You clutch frantically at the person next to you, and you sigh with relief when it's all over—then buy a ticket and stand in line for the next trip.

The thing to keep in mind about a roller coaster is that it's a manufactured experience. Trained engineers carefully plan every hairpin turn, every death drop, every slow-down and speed-up to produce the precise effect you're feeling as you hurtle along.

Just as the engineer plans the roller-coaster rider's thrills, so, too, does the suspense writer calculate and produce the effects her writing induces in her readers. Some writers dislike being reminded that they're in charge of creating the reader's experience. They prefer to think of the characters as taking over and writing the story, or they like to believe that an unseen hand reaches in and makes the story work.

Perhaps when you've written eight to ten books, your subconscious mind *can* take over and produce a state-of-the-art thrill ride of a novel, but I think letting your unconscious write your books is like asking a group of nine-year-olds to design the next roller coaster at Disney World. The kids know what they like, but only a real pro can create that experience for them.

A Little Suspense History

If the mystery genre has one parent in Edgar Allan Poe, then suspense fiction has both a mother and a father. The mother of suspense fiction is the gothic novel best represented by Charlotte Brontë's *Jane Eyre*, and its father is the spy novel, early examples of which are Erskine Chalders's *The Riddle of the Sands* and W. Somerset Maugham's Ashenden stories.

Gothic Roots

Before Brontë there was Mrs. Radcliffe, whose *Mysteries of Udolpho* figures in Jane Austen's gothic parody, *Northanger Abbey*. The early gothics featured ghosts, haunted houses, and mysteries from the past, and were heavy on atmosphere and passion. The heroine was a woman alone, without family to help her, and she was in love with a man whose cryptic cruelty toward her only fueled the flame of her desire. The emphasis was on the personal and the emotional, the setting was a single house with a troubled past, and the heroine's bravery often earned her the love of the unavailable man at the heart of the mystery. Wilkie Collins's *The Woman in White* and *The Moonstone* are at heart gothics with elements of police procedure (which was very new at the time) thrown in.

Espionage Roots

The spy genre took a very different approach. The problem presented wasn't one of a single woman and a single man in a single house; it involved the fate of the entire free world. Like the gothic heroine, the spy never knows whom to trust, but unlike her, he's been thrust into a larger world and must operate within the customs of various countries. Even though there's one protagonist we care about, there are usually several other characters whose viewpoints we see and whose plotlines we follow until they converge for the final confrontation/crisis. Personal crisis and individual emotion were very far down on the list of priorities in this kind of book—until John Le Carré wrote *The Spy Who Came in from the Cold.*

Suspense Today

Most of today's suspense novels arise out of one or the other of these traditions. Romantic suspense, relationship suspense, romantic intrigue, suspense with supernatural overtones all derive from gothic forebears. Thrillers, whether medical, techno, political, or international intrigue, are all variants on the spy genre because they involve issues larger than the emotional lives of individuals. One hallmark of both strands of the suspense skein is the ordinary person thrust by forces beyond her control into a larger world that she doesn't understand.

Descendants of the Gothic Tradition

Just as the modern category known as "Regency Romance" follows the template laid down by Jane Austen in *Pride and Prejudice*, the classic gothic mirrors *Jane Eyre.* A young woman comes, alone, to a big house in a remote and very picturesque location. She is a governess, a poor relation, a servant, a ward—someone powerless and without friends or family to turn to.

The owner of the house is a mercurial man with oversized moods. The girl dislikes him, fears him, slowly grows to like and then love him, and all the time mysterious events have her wondering what evil lurks in the house. If there are children, her duty is to protect them from this man, and from the dread secret he hides.

Dread secrets will be revealed. The man will confess his love and explain why he can't return her love even though he has feelings for her. She will bring light into this dark place and free him from his past. He will raise her to his own social level. Sunlight will pour through the narrow gothic windows of the old house and the shadow will be dispelled forever.

You think this genre died in 1945?

Think again. Victoria Holt, Barbara Michaels, and Ruth Rendell writing as Barbara Vine have done very well with it, adapting the classic form to more modern times yet retaining its emphasis on atmosphere and setting.

Romantic Suspense

So strong is this subgenre that while I was waiting for a plane, I walked into the airport bookstore and found that eight out of ten of the best-selling titles were essentially romantic suspense reads. A woman comes home to a small town from the big city for some reason: lost job, divorce, widowhood. She finds a place to live and meets friends, but mysterious, disturbing things begin to happen. She's threatened and she doesn't know why. Her presence has stirred up old ghosts. Menacing phone calls, strange sounds in the night, people she thought she knew making cryptic but clearly hostile remarks—and she has no idea why.

In most romantic suspense, the writer gives her protagonist a choice of two (at least) men vying for her attentions. One is considerate, respectable, helpful, supportive, kind, and available. The other is argumentative, disreputable, obstructionist, contrary, rude, and withholding.

Guess which one is Prince Charming?

You've got it: Mr. Rude Guy is her knight in shining armor, the one who is really on her side even if he acts like he's not. Mr. Nice Guy turns out to be the bad guy, the one who's trying to drive her out of town, the one whose daddy killed her daddy back in the past, or the one who's cheating her out of her inheritance.

Our heroine not only has to show her moxie by sticking around in a dangerous situation and her cleverness in unraveling the secrets and lies, she has to prove her ability to judge people by (finally) realizing which of her suitors is really meant for her.

"Romantic intrigue" takes this basic template and adds international spy elements to it. This time hero and heroine play out their drama against the backdrop of world events. M. M. Kaye's series of books featuring exotic locales in the titles are great examples, and this kind of story is the mainstay of the Harlequin Romantic Intrigue line.

Relationship Suspense

Can a woman find happiness in a suspense novel if she's already married? Are her days as a suspense heroine over? Ask Daphne du Maurier, whose *Rebecca* set the tone for a subgenre I call "relationship suspense."

Rebecca brings its nameless heroine to Manderley, a big seaside house on the rocky coast of Cornwall that would be very much at home in a gothic romance. The house itself, along with its sinister housekeeper, Mrs. Danvers, provides a great deal of the atmosphere that makes the book so compelling. The heroine is in a hostile environment and the only person she can trust is her new husband.

But can she trust him? Does he regret marrying her because she can never measure up to the dead Rebecca, his first wife?

Our relationship suspense heroine is married, but did her husband marry her for love or money? She swings between both views, alternately worrying that she's about to be killed for her inheritance and reassuring herself that he loves her for herself alone. It's as if she married both Mr. Rude Guy and Mr. Nice Guy rolled into a single character. The issue for her: Which one is her real husband?

Even without wealth and great houses, fear that a marriage is not what the wife thinks it is makes for a compelling story. Marilyn Wallace's *So Shall You Reap* examines a Hudson Valley wife's increasing doubts about her husband in a modern variation on the gothic tradition. *See Jane Run*, by Joy Fielding, is a fast-paced, intense psychological study of an amnesic woman with a husband she can't remember whether to trust.

Personal Jeopardy

Personal jeopardy is at the heart of most gothic-tradition suspense novels. A child is kidnapped, a woman is stalked, a man is targeted by very bad dudes for reasons he can't explain. An ordinary person must pit his or her entire being against powerful enemies, and the suspense lies in whether or not our hero will survive and prevail. The person in jeopardy is not always the protagonist; parents become heroes to rescue their children, a husband or wife fights for a spouse captured by the enemy.

The key is the struggle, the David-and-Goliath confrontation in which a person very much like ourselves must become braver, stronger, more heroic in order to win the unequal fight. Watching the transformation from victim to victor is the heart of the reader's joy in this kind of book.

Why is this ordinary person suddenly the target of Really Bad Dudes?

Sometimes the protagonist made bad choices. The young lawyer in *The Firm* chose to work at The Firm not knowing the full truth about his new employers. In other books ghosts from the past come thundering into the present, as happens in Carla Neggers's romantic suspense novels. A child is kidnapped for ransom, or a wife is held captive to put pressure on the husband. Alfred Hitchcock's *The Man Who Knew Too Much* put James Stewart's life (and that of his wife and child) in danger because he heard a man's dying words—even though he had no idea what those words meant. Ignorance is no defense in the world of personal jeopardy.

Jan Burke turned the tables on "husband rescues kidnapped wife" by having her reporter-hero Irene Kelly free her police officer husband in *Hocus* (he'd already done the same for her in *Dear Irene*). Worse than being in jeopardy oneself is having one's child in jeopardy. Judith Kelman, Meg O'Brien, and Aljean Harmetz have all covered that heart-stopping territory in their suspense novels.

What all these subgenres have in common is that the immediate danger is limited to a single person, a family, a small unit within the larger world. Even the fanatics who plan to blow up the Texas state legislature in Mary Willis Walker's *All the Dead Lie Down* won't wipe out more than a city block or so if they succeed. The world is not at stake.

Spy Fiction Offshoots

In spy fiction, the world *is* at stake. The danger has implications for entire countries, not just the protagonist and her immediate family.

There's an abstract quality to spy fiction that arises out of that fact. If I tell you 5,000 children a month are killed in the United States, you're shocked but not emotionally engaged. If I start telling you about the child in northern San Diego who's been missing for two weeks, if I show you her school picture and the video of her running through the garden hose-spray on a summer afternoon, you'll feel pity and sadness. (In fact, since I wrote those words, her burned body was found in the woods and you probably saw the news on television and can perhaps recall her name even now.) One child captures our attention far more than a mass of children.

That's human nature. So one challenge for the spy branch of the suspense tree is to make the conflict personal without losing the big-picture impact of its high stakes. Giving the reader a character to identify with at every turn helps a lot. Don't just tell us a bad apple in the CIA barrel is about to rat out our man in Moscow; introduce us to that man so we will grieve his death and hate the traitor for causing it.

Even before the end of the Cold War, new variations on the spy novel made their way onto the shelves, using the old format but offering insights into other kinds of large organizations at war with one another and endangering masses of people.

Suspense vs. Thriller

What makes a suspense novel a thriller?

My facetious answer used to be, "A six-figure advance," but I've come to see that it's more than that. Yes, thrillers are big sellers, but they also take the reader to a higher level than an "ordinary" suspense novel. Thriller writers aren't afraid to take their plots, characters, situations, and locales to the max, pushing the envelope of credibility at every possible turn. They pile it on, pitting their protagonists against super-powerful enemies and putting obstacle upon obstacle in the way of success. They squeeze everything they can out of their settings, to the point where the reader ends up knowing more than he ever wanted to know about the internal workings of submarines or dinosaur DNA.

And yet that's part of the thrill inherent in the thriller: the sense of getting more than you bargained for, of being taken inside the inner circle and told things no one is supposed to know. Just when you think the plot can't possibly take one more twist, it throws one more monkey wrench into the hero's plans and spins your head around. It takes you to the highest highs and the lowest lows, and if it does these things at the expense of credibility and ordinary human emotion—well, that's what you want when you're sitting in a plane traveling cross-country, isn't it? (Unless, of course, you're reading Michael Crichton's *Airframe*.) You want something to rivet your eyes to the page, to let you escape into an exciting, danger-filled place.

The thriller is just one facet of the jewel that is suspense, but it's a powerful one in the eyes of publishers in love with the bottom line. Thriller subgenres dominate the best-seller's list, and each presents the reader with its own special pleasures.

The Techno-Thriller

This is Tom Clancy territory; he began his career with *The Hunt for Red October*, making the high-tech submarine a vital part of the plot and giving so much technical detail that you could practically build your own once you put down the book. For every reader who skipped over the specs section of the book, there seemed to be two others who wanted more.

Many techno-thrillers are based on what-if horror stories about technology gone awry. In fact, one aspect of the thriller market in general is its fascination with "systems gone mad"—we'll see that medical thrillers focus on medical technology gone mad, legal thrillers zero in on the law gone mad, and so forth. In one sense, they're all rewriting *Frankenstein*, and the only reason they aren't found in the science fiction section of the bookstore is that they purport to be about the present or the very immediate future.

The theme, as exemplified perfectly by Michael Crichton's *Jurassic Park* and its sequels, is that man is too flawed to be trusted with overly ambitious scientific projects. In other words, man shouldn't play God by restoring extinct species to life. Even with the best motives in the world, evil will prevail in the end because hubris, that old human failing, always corrupts.

The danger in writing a techno-thriller is falling in love with technology and forgetting to thrill. A second pitfall is making the technology more interesting than the characters. Remember, readers still have to identify with a living, breathing human being with a goal. Even if the story demands a large cast, the writer needs to narrow the focus to a small number of major characters whose destinies become important to the reader. It's vital that the big-picture writers create a hierarchy of characters and tell the reader up front which are the main characters.

Medical Thrillers

Robin Cook's *Coma* is the prototype here. Unscrupulous doctors are harvesting organs from healthy people in order to keep rich people supplied with substitute organs.

Other medical thrillers involve rampant diseases (Richard Preston's *The Hot Zone*), and abuses of reproductive technology (Tess Garritsen's *Life Support*). All these plotlines play upon an inherent fear of doctors and their ability to save and destroy life—and the fear that these enormous powers, used for evil instead of good, will destroy humanity as surely as those revived dinosaurs.

Political Thrillers

Richard North Patterson takes issues that burn in the public mind and shows how they resonate in the lives of very important political figures. In *No Safe Place*, a Robert F. Kennedy–like candidate runs for office, haunted by the death of his older brother. *Protect and Serve* introduces a female candidate for the Supreme Court caught on the horns of the abortion dilemma and a John McCain–like senator who must choose between painful personal revelations and political principle.

Crime Thrillers

One relatively new suspense form is the serial killer novel, a cross between near-horror and police procedural. The horror isn't based on the existence of vampires, or ghosts, or paranormal phenomena, but on the very real horror engendered by true-life killers. Yet the emotional impact on the reader is similar: being scared out of one's wits. The police procedural angle allows the brain to be engaged and a level of understanding to be reached. While many serial killer books are published each year, none have had more impact than Thomas Harris's *Red Dragon*, which was the first to reveal the secrets of the FBI's profiling unit.

The key to *Red Dragon* for me wasn't just the amazing and enthralling look into the world of profilers, but the way Harris humanized the serial killer by showing us his horrific childhood. This has become a cliché, but it was powerful when new, and it said something ordinary civilians hadn't really understood before. Patricia Cornwell's books offer a similar backstage look at the autopsy, creating a hybrid form that might be called "procedural suspense."

Legal Thrillers

The world of the legal thriller is an interesting one. Very seldom is there as much at stake in these as there is in the techno and medical subgenres. Humanity itself is not in jeopardy, and usually, only one life is on the line and the life isn't always that of the lawyer protagonist. Yet the legal thriller continues its commercial reign. What is it about this form that keeps readers coming back for more?

The legal thriller combines the straight suspense novel, with its emphasis on the protagonist's personal danger, with the courtroom drama, which traditionally focused on other people's troubles.

What do I mean by this? Take the best courtroom novel ever. (Yes, if you read it today you'll think it's amazingly slow-paced. It's not a thriller. Never was. Never wanted to be.) *Anatomy of a Murder* shows us a criminal trial from beginning to end, and one of its most striking features is that the trial itself doesn't begin until Midpoint, halfway through the book.

That's because the author, Robert Traver, who was a lawyer and judge in Michigan, knew what most non-lawyers at that time didn't: that a trial really begins the moment a criminal lawyer meets his client. The lawyer, consciously or unconsciously, sums up his client and his client's situation and begins mentally writing his summation to the jury. In this case, attorney Paul Biegler wants very much to believe that his client killed his wife's rapist in a moment of temporary insanity, or, as Michigan courts demand it be worded, irresistible impulse.

The first half of the book consists of preparation for trial, the second half of the trial itself. This is a common feature of courtroom novels now, but today's thrillers add a lot more personal baggage to the lawyer-hero and often put her in dire jeopardy over and above winning or losing the case.

At the trial, things go wrong. Witnesses lie and deny they ever told the lawyer a different story. The judge rules against the lawyer, keeping out lines of questioning or barring witnesses that she needs to win the case. Just when things look blackest, a witness comes forward, or a previous witness changes her story and tells the truth, and our hero makes a stunning summation to the jury and wins the case. Justice prevails even against institutionalized corruption.

John Grisham added a major new twist to the genre with *The Firm*. Here the lawyer wasn't engaged in other people's troubles; he was trying to save his own life. There was no courtroom drama; the entire story unfolded outside of the court system and involved a very nasty law firm's machinations to keep a renegade young lawyer from telling all to the authorities. Law, in fact, played very little part in the story. The tale could just as easily have been set in a bank or a multinational corporation or a police department; any organization capable of being totally tainted by Mafia connections would have done as well.

Instead of the hero-lawyer engaged in a symbolic duel with his counterpart on the other side of the legal divide, Grisham's hero stood against a vast array of conspirators with immense, shadowy power. He never knew when he was speaking to someone with connections back to The Firm, and even the FBI couldn't be trusted to protect him and to treat him with decency. In the end, a small outlaw band turns the tables on The Firm and manages to escape the clutches of both the bad guys and the so-called good guys.

Writers like John Lescroart and Steve Martini use the legal thriller to explore complex psychological relationships and legal-political machinations. Their defense lawyer heroes fight for justice for their accused clients, while prosecutors star in Chris Darden's Nikki Hill series and in Nancy Taylor Rosenberg's legal thrillers.

Crimes and Capers

One final branch of the suspense tree is the novel written from the point of view of the criminal. These can be psychological studies (James Ellroy's *Killer on the Road*, Donald Westlake's *The Ax*), step-by-step accounts of intricately planned crimes that depend on nerves of steel and split-second timing (*Void Moon* by Michael Connelly), or slice-of-life glimpses into the lives of low-level criminals with colorful vocabularies (books by Elmore Leonard, Carl Hiaasen).

The difference between these novels and the usual suspense read is that this time our sympathy is engaged on behalf of someone who isn't innocent. We like the crooks in *Get Shorty* better than the so-called honest citizens of Hollywood, and we root for the gangs that couldn't shoot straight because they make us laugh. In the lighter side of this subgenre, humor softens the suspense edge, but the structure is the same as in the spy novel. Many characters with different goals and separate paths step onto the road of life and by the end of the book, all the paths will collide, all the characters will interact in surprising ways, accidents will happen, and no one in the book will emerge unscathed by the experience.

Reading a well-written caper novel is like watching those guys who used to balance spinning plates on the *Ed Sullivan Show*. Your eyes dart from one plate to the next, watching one wobble and then sighing with relief as the juggler balances it again.

Whichever subcategory of the suspense novel you prefer, the key is to give the reader the roller-coaster experience of intense highs, deep lows, terrifying twists, and a satisfying conclusion to the ride.

6. Myths and Dreams

Basic Ingredients of Suspense Fiction

ONCE UPON a time, there was a girl named Snow White. She was as good as she was pretty, but her father married a woman who was jealous of Snow White's beauty. The Wicked Queen who was her stepmother tried several times to get rid of Snow White, and she finally sent the girl into the woods with a huntsman who had orders to kill Snow White and bring her heart back to the Wicked Queen.

Now there's a suspense tale! Our innocent heroine, who has no idea why all this enmity is directed at her, steps into the dark, unfriendly woods with a professional animal slaughterer against whom she has no weapons at all. How can this end well?

No weapons except her innate goodness, and the beauty that is the outward manifestation of that goodness. Her goodness wins over the Huntsman, who kills a deer instead of Snow White, and brings the deer's heart back to the W.Q. as proof that Snow White is dead at last.

Snow White, meanwhile, is still in the deep, dark woods with no shelter and no friends, no coat, nothing. What will happen to this innocent heroine? Who will help her?

Seven dwarfs, of course. Again, her goodness prevails over their grumpy resistance to taking her in (Disney gave us one Grumpy; the Grimms had all the dwarfs acting pretty inhospitable at first). She wins them over with her cheerful willingness to cook and clean for them, her singing and her love of nature.

She's safe at last, hidden from the Wicked Queen who thinks she's dead. Right?

Wrong. The W.Q. has a secret weapon in the form of the traitorous Magic Mirror. "Mirror, mirror on the wall/Who's the fairest of them all?"

"It's still Snow White and she's hiding in the woods with seven little bearded guys, so if you want to be the fairest, you'll have to knock her off."

This time the W.Q. is too smart to trust any huntsmen because she sees that they'll be blinded by Snow White's beauty and goodness, so she goes to the woods herself, disguised as a kindly old lady, and takes a poisoned apple for her stepdaughter to eat.

I was a kid when the Disney version came to my town; the Wicked Queen was my first movie villain and I still remember that apple. It was half-red and half-green and it seemed to shine from the screen like a Christmas bauble. The entire kid audience shouted, "Don't eat it!" when Snow White reached for it, only she didn't hear us, so she took that apple and the kindly old lady morphed into the Wicked Queen and there were probably a few wet beds in Toledo, Ohio, that night.

See, that's my theory of suspense: that it all begins in fairy tale, with the very first stories we ever learned. And those stories weren't cleaned up and politically corrected when I was five or six; they were the hard-core Grimm stuff with hearts ripped out of bodies and pure evil trying to crush pure innocence.

Rites of Passage

All fairy tales are rites of passage, mystical handbooks teaching us how to change and grow, how to travel to a new place in life, how to prevail over the forces of darkness within and without. They all have certain elements in common, no matter what cultural background they come from.

There is a problem, usually caused by some turmoil within the home. A woodsman marries a second wife who wants his children dead, a young girl's father remarries and the new wife brings wicked stepsisters into her life, a mermaid falls in love with a prince who walks on two legs.

The fairy-tale hero is cast out and alone. She finds helpers and guides along the way. The birds guide Hansel and Gretel back to their home; mice become coach horses for Cinderella's carriage. Ants help Psyche separate seeds from sand. Elders such as the seven dwarfs or the old woman who lives in the stilt house guide the hero to new ways of thinking.

The middle of the story involves tasks and tests, lessons and learning.

Snow White first "tames" the huntsman whose mission is to kill her, and then she "tames" the dwarfs by bringing the joys of domesticity to their cabin. Hansel twice finds ways to guide himself and Gretel back home, failing only when the birds eat the trail of breadcrumbs the third time. Then he and Gretel fool the old witch into thinking Hansel is losing weight by substituting a twig for Hansel's finger, and Gretel passes the ultimate test when she tosses the old witch into her own oven.

Death is confronted directly. The still-beating heart of the deer in the huntsman's hand is a graphic reminder to Snow White of what might have been. Gretel's casting the witch into the flames meant to cook her brother, Sleeping Beauty's long deathlike coma, Snow White's seeming death from the poisoned apple—all are symbolic of the death of the immature being and the rebirth of the new, mature, tested hero who has traveled to a new state in life.

The marriage at the end of so many fairy tales is described by scholars as a Sacred Marriage of the masculine and feminine within a single human being. Looked at this way, the Prince Charmings are more than door prizes, they represent the state of readiness for adulthood and the new strength the heroine gained by undergoing the tests.

The pure-evil villain forces the hero to change and grow. But for all those wicked stepmothers, our heroes would stay at home with Daddy, never venturing out and testing themselves, never maturing from girl to woman.

What does all this have to do with suspense fiction written by and for adults? Let's look at one writer who has captured the essence of fairy tale in her suspense stories and see how closely the elements conform to a classic tale.

A Cry in the Night, Mary Higgins Clark

Once upon a time, there was a little mermaid who lived under the sea. She met a handsome prince and fell in love with him, but he was a land-dwelling creature and couldn't live in her world. So she made a bargain with a magician who promised to change her from mermaid to woman: she could have legs and breathe on land, but she would lose her voice and be unable to speak.

She made the deal and won her prince, but she didn't live happily ever after, not in the Hans Christian Andersen original. The prince treated her badly and she couldn't go back to her home in the sea because she'd given up that part of herself for him. So she wasted away, and her statue looks out over Copenhagen Harbor as a reminder to all women to keep the essence of who they are and not sacrifice everything for love of a man.

Once upon a time in Manhattan there lived a single mother with two children. One day while taking her kids home from day care, wearing an old sweater, she met Prince Charming, who wore a camel's-hair coat and silk scarf and had Viking good looks. He fell in love with Jenny McPartland at once and began showering her with gifts, which the young mother appreciated because she was an orphan twice over, having lost her parents when she was a child and having just buried the grandmother who raised her.

This part sounds a lot like Cinderella, doesn't it? Now comes the Little Mermaid part.

The prince woos the young woman in a whirlwind courtship and marries her, whisking her away to his hometown in the Midwest, creating what she calls a "magical transformation" of her life. Instead of old clothes and cheap sweaters, she has all the designer outfits she can wear. Instead of her children wearing hand-me-downs and going to day care, they can ride horses and have her company full time, and what's more, the prince loves them so much he wants to adopt them and put their feckless father out of their lives for good.

Oh, there are a few little signs and portents, but in true fairy-tale fashion, our heroine talks herself out of seeing anything wrong, which is very much a part of the early stage in the mystical transformation from unaware child to aware adulthood.

What are the signs and portents? The prince's extreme jealousy of our heroine's ex-husband, for one thing. He actually throws away a perfectly good meatloaf our heroine wants to serve for dinner because the ex touched it. (The ex doesn't like the prince either, but we tend to discount that because our fairy-tale-raised hearts want to believe that the prince is a prince and not a huntsman.)

Still. A perfectly good meatloaf. And that's not all—our prince has a way of throwing quite childish tantrums when things don't go exactly his way. And then we learn that the prince was married before, that he has a painting of his dead wife that is almost an icon, and—here comes the biggie—*he wants the heroine to wear his dead wife's nightgown on their wedding night!*

Are we getting the feeling our mermaid made a bad deal when she left her nice comfortable ocean to be with this guy?

How about her lost voice? How does our Manhattan mermaid become unable to speak because she made a bargain with a magician to win her prince?

This book begins with a prologue showing our heroine on her way to the prince's secret cabin in the woods (okay, we're sneaking into Bluebeard territory here) to open the Door That Must Not Be Opened. She has tools with her, obviously intended to effect her entry into the cabin, and as she passes the winter-bare trees she nails bits of cloth to them for markers so she can find her way back (recalling Hansel and Gretel). As she walks she thinks about going to the sheriff: "But he would surely refuse to help and would simply stare at her with that familiar look of speculative disdain."

The town belongs to the prince. Any time she voices the slightest doubts about the prince or raises a question about the dead wife, she's met with the same blank stares, the same robotic assurance that there's nothing wrong. As far as making herself heard, she might as well have no voice because nothing she says is listened to or acted on. (Of course, being from Manhattan makes her doubly suspect.)

The worst part is that her own daughters stop listening to her. They love their new house and new life and the horses and the kindly prince and to them our heroine begins to seem like a wicked stepmother intent on depriving them of joy.

This time the Little Mermaid *can* undo the bad bargain she made. Borrowing from Bluebeard's brave wife, she opens the Door That Must Not Be Opened and lets all the secrets out, and that power is what allows her, at long last, to be heard. That and one very unexpected ally: the ex-husband (just think of him as the dwarf who got away).

The Hero's Journey

Joseph Campbell died in 1987. He's not writing movies in Hollywood, but sometimes it seems as if his spirit infuses many screenwriting classes these days. Whether it's an interior journey like the one in *A Beautiful Mind* or a blockbuster explosion-riddled thriller like *Independence Day*, we love seeing the hero's journey over and over again.

What is the journey, and how does it inform suspense writing?

The Hero's Journey

- Ordinary world
- Call to adventure
  (10-minute hook)

- Refusal of the call
- Meeting the mentor
- Taking the adventure
- Crossing the first threshold into special world
  (End of Arc One)

- Tests
- Tasks
- Alliances
- Enemies
- Approach to the Inmost Cave
  (End of Arc Two; could be Midpoint)

- Ordeal
- Brush with death
  (Alternative Midpoint at end of Arc Three)

- Loss of an ally
- Revelation of a turncoat (in Arc Three)
- Confrontation with opponent (climax)
- Death of a villain
- Reward: seizing the sword

- The road back
- Return to ordinary world with elixir
- Coda: ordinary world transformed by the journey

Our hero begins his journey in the ordinary world. This is Cinderella's house before her father remarries, or, in T. Jefferson Parker's *Little Saigon*, hero Chuck Fry's world before his brother's wife is kidnapped. Some external event forces change and decision, and pushes the hero out of the ordinary world into a special world where new realities, new rules, must be learned, and where there will be tests and tasks to be mastered.

The Little Mermaid's special world is our ordinary one, because her ordinary world lies under the sea. Clark's heroine is taken from her ordinary world of Manhattan to the special world of her prince's domain; Fry's special world is that of the Vietnamese exiles. Even though they live in Orange County, California, and he makes no physical journey to find them, their world is alien to him. Accepting the adventure and crossing into the special world marks the end of Arc One and the beginning of the big bad middle.

The middle of the story is where the growth occurs. Here the hero meets allies and learns to distinguish (through trial and error) between those he can trust and those he can't. Tests and tasks abound, skills are learned, a mentor gives direction (in *Little Saigon* a Vietnamese elder helps Fry understand some of what's going on), and the hero moves inexorably toward a direct confrontation with evil.

Evil may reach out and harm the hero, but eventually, he must move in the direction of the evil instead of running away. Once freed from police custody, the Fugitive (in the movie of the same name) doesn't hop a plane and go to Peru, he marches straight into the very hospital where he once practiced, risking being seen and captured, in order to find the one-armed man. When the Wizard of Oz tells Dorothy to get a straw from the Wicked Witch's broomstick, she doesn't shrug and say, "I guess I can't get home then"; she sets off toward the witch's castle to do what has to be done. When Clark's mermaid finds out about The Door That Must Not Be Opened, she steels herself to open it, no matter what the consequences. The cops, the Vietnamese, and Fry's own brother and father all beg him to stay out of the kidnapping case, but he doggedly continues his quest for the truth that will free his sister-in-law.

These heroes enter the Inmost Cave, the most dangerous place they can be, the heart of their enemy's power, because they must. And they encounter death. Snow White "dies" when she eats the poisoned apple; Jenny McPartland is urged to "become" her dead predecessor; Fry faces death when he's pitted against ruthless Vietnamese gangsters.

The ultimate confrontation pits good against evil. Good wins, but we're never quite sure it's going to, and we never know exactly how our innocent and seemingly less powerful hero will find the tools and the heart to prevail.

What heroes win is the elixir, a fancy name for their new knowledge, their hard-won insights and maturity. In *A Cry in the Night*, it's the knowledge that our heroine, like the Little Mermaid, gave up too much of herself for her prince. In *Little Saigon*, the elixir is Fry's reconciliation with his family.

In some books, there's also a sacred marriage. Not only has Clark's heroine escaped her Bluebeard of a prince, but the local vet will make a wonderful real prince and he won't ask her to wear another woman's identity in order to be loved.

Well, okay, that's a chick book. How does all this fairy-tale stuff fit into a suspense novel with masculine energy?

Little Saigon, T. Jefferson Parker

Once upon a time there were three brothers, and the youngest was called Simple.

Actually, in this book there are two brothers. The older, Bennett, is a Vietnam veteran, brave and strong, his father's right-hand man, responsible and married to a beautiful Vietnamese woman. He's the hero, right?

Wrong. His younger brother, Chuck, the family screw-up, the second-best surfer in Laguna Beach (that second-best theme is going to come up again), the boy who caused his little sister's drowning, the man who lives in a cave-house and runs a tacky surf shop instead of working in the family business—he's the hero and it's his transition from aging boy to mature man that we're going to experience.

Chuck goes through the same maturation process as Jenny McPartland. He's tested by the search for his sister-in-law; he meets a mysterious woman with secrets of her own and has to decide whether to trust her or not; he's helped by an elder in the Vietnamese community, and then that elder is murdered before his eyes.

By the end of the book, he's become a man instead of a boy; he's matched his heroic brother in his ability to go head-to-head with vicious, violent killers and emerge triumphant. Without the testing process, he'd still be second best.

The Night Manager, John Le Carré

Here's a perfect example of the middlebook as training ground. The title character begins the story as the night manager of a hotel in Cairo. When someone he cares about is ruthlessly killed by bad guys, he lets himself be recruited by British intelligence. His decision to join the team is Plot Point One and his training and first tasks comprise Arc Two.

Arc Two takes the character from raw recruit status to the successful completion of the first task, which also sets up his cover for the ultimate goal, infiltrating the Big Bad Guy's entourage. Task two takes our hero from England to Canada and further away from his ordinary world. By the time he creates the scenario that allows him entry into the world of the Big Bad Guy, we believe that a man whose biggest concern used to be whether or not the presidential suite was ready is capable of bringing down the Big Bad Guy because we've seen him master smaller but still impressive tasks. He's earned the right to play the big time.

Arc Three gives us the infiltration itself. Now he's in the Cave, in this case the tropical island compound and yacht belonging to the Big Bad Guy. He's in a great position to grab up all the secrets and blow this guy's world apart, and all he has to do is not be found out because the moment he's found out, he's a dead man. Every cocktail party, every walk on the beach, is fraught because allies of the Big Bad Guy don't trust him and are working to expose him.

Then he falls in love with the Big Bad Guy's girlfriend. He's in the frying pan already, and Le Carré turns up the heat.

Psyche's Journey to Hades

The kinds of tests and tasks the hero performs in the middle of a suspense novel resemble the ordeal a goddess of ancient Greece devised for her disobedient daughter-in-law.

Once upon a time there was a girl named Psyche. She was very pretty and nice, but she was a mortal, so when Eros, the god of love, fell for her, his mother, Aphrodite, wasn't thrilled. And when your mother-in-law is a goddess, you'd better watch your step.

In order to hide his godliness from his new bride, Eros told Psyche she was never to look at him in daylight. They made love in the dark, and Eros crept away to sleep alone afterwards. Psyche's sisters thought this was strange, and they urged her to get a glimpse of her husband in case he looked like the Elephant Man or something. So one night Psyche crept into the chamber where Eros slept and held a candle close to his face. She was relieved to find that he was wonderfully handsome, but she stood gazing at him for too long, because the candle dripped hot wax on his face and woke him up.

Eros felt betrayed and walked out on his bride. Aphrodite told him it was no more than he should have expected, marrying an outsider. Psyche was devastated. She cried and mourned, realizing that she should have trusted her man, and she begged the gods to find a way to return Eros to her.

After a suitable period of self-flagellation, Psyche finally got Aphrodite to agree that Eros might come back to her—if and when she completed a few little tasks. Nothing too hard, mind you, just tokens of her good faith.

Task One: Separate the Seeds

The first task sounds easy enough. Psyche is given a bushel of seeds and told to separate them into poppy seeds, sesame seeds, etc. However, not only is the task difficult, but in addition, she is given an impossible time limit because the seeds are so many and so tiny. But Psyche gets help from an army of ants, who quickly divide the seeds into different piles.

The lessons of this task: the art of fine distinctions, of separating seeds, is a metaphor for being able to tell truth from lies, false friends from true. The ants are symbolic, too. Small helpers, people or things that seem insignificant and powerless, can become the best friends a suspense hero ever had.

Task Two: The Golden Fleece

"Get me some golden fleece from the golden rams," orders Aphrodite. This is a task that daunted Jason, and he had boats and men at his command. How is one woman supposed to face charging rams and get their fleece?

Answer: by thinking like a woman instead of a man. Psyche comes to see that she doesn't have to confront the rams to get their fleece. What she needs to do is put them to sleep with beautiful music and then creep into the field and take the fleece while they're unaware of her.

When I say "think like a woman," I don't mean that it's impossible for a female hero to pick up the sword and face danger head-on, only that if you don't *have* to face it head-on, what's wrong with an alternate approach that still gets you what you want? Psyche fulfills the task through intelligence instead of brute force; music soothes the savage beasts and allows her to take what she wants without shedding any blood, human or animal.

Similarly, the suspense hero learns to get information in ways other than simply pulling a gun on someone. Subtlety and intelligence prove mightier weapons than brute force and direct confrontation.

Task Three: Go to Hell

Aphrodite saves the best for last. Having watched her daughter-in-law separate the seeds and obtain the golden fleece, she now sets a task she's certain Psyche can't do. She orders Psyche to go into the dark realm ruled by Hades in order to get her some makeup used by Hades's wife, Persephone.

There are a few rules about going into the ancient Greek version of hell.

The first is that you have to pay the ferryman, Charon. The second is that you have to get past the famous three-headed dog guarding the gates. And you'd better not eat anything while you're there or you'll have to stay forever. The hardest thing Psyche must do is to refuse the many beggars she meets along the way. The truth is that they are beyond her help; if she reaches out, she'll fail in her quest. So setting limits is part of the final task and test.

Going through a symbolic death by visiting the Underworld is a major theme of suspense novels. Our hero is tested to the max and emerges from her deathlike state a stronger woman, one who is now worthy of her god-husband.

The next time you pick up a suspense novel, play a game with yourself and see how many fairy-tale elements you recognize. In Mary Higgins Clark's *A Stranger Is Watching*, she gives us a climax in the bowels of Grand Central Station—about as Inmost Cave–like as you can get. A bag lady gives our heroine vital information—and doesn't she remind you of the gnomic old witches of legend?

Spymasters are mentors; allies who turn into enemies are shape-shifters; the well-meaning friends who discourage our hero from pursuing the adventure are threshold guardians; and that diamond necklace handed down through the generations makes a very nice treasure.

And you can't tell me that Clarice Starling didn't play Beauty to Hannibal Lecter's Beast in *Silence of the Lambs*, or that her brave decision to go after serial killer Buffalo Bill wasn't the act of a modern Perseus heading into the Labyrinth to kill the Minotaur.

Myth lives.

7. Build Me an Arc, II
The Structure of the Suspense Novel

ONCE UPON a time—not the world's worst opening line, is it? Let fairy-tale and hero's-journey elements act as your suspense template, and you'll hook the child in all your readers. The thing is, most of the early material in a suspense novel consists of setting up characters and situations that will pay off in the last half of the book. The question for the writer: how to keep setup from becoming mechanical and boring?

Let's take a look at *Hostage* by Robert Crais. It's a fast-paced thriller that pulls out all the stops for a state-of-the-art roller-coaster ride, and it's a good example of how to put suspense on every page.

The Prologue

Crais opens with a prologue, and it is a true prologue, meaning that it shows us a scene that takes place before the action of the novel begins. That, after all, is what the *pro* in prologue means, but it isn't always what writers do. Some writers pull an exciting scene out of the middle of the book, stick it in the front, and then write their way toward the events of the so-called prologue.

It's cheating. I did it in *Fresh Kills* and I'd do it again if I had to (and I had to for a very common mystery reason, namely that the victim refused to die and I had eight chapters before the first body dropped. Unacceptable, so I put a finding-the-body scene up front to let the readers know that the character was doomed. It would be better if the body dropped earlier, or if the plot contained sufficient suspense for the "prologue" to be unnecessary, but failing those things, something had to be done to keep the reader's interest.) Still, it's cheating. It's not a true prologue, and it's a stopgap measure taking the place of true in-the-moment suspense.

But Crais's opening in *Hostage* is a true prologue, which gives us the opportunity to explore its uses.

The main character, Jeff Talley, is a hostage negotiator for the LAPD at the time the prologue takes place. He's negotiating with a crazed husband who's threatening to shoot his hostages, and he's deathly afraid that he's blown the case.

He has.

He's blown this case and someone dies, which will haunt him throughout the rest of the book, and he's so burned out that even thinking about his own wife and daughter can't bring him back to life. He's an empty shell.

This prologue comes under the heading of "establishing the character's ghost of the past," or "how a trained expert hostage negotiator burned out in the big city and ended up in a one-horse suburb where he will, *of course*, face a much bigger, much worse, much more challenging hostage situation and be afraid he can't handle it."

In other words, it's setup. It creates deep doubt in the reader about the ability of the main character to deal with the stress of another hostage negotiation, and any reader with a brain will realize that the entire rest of the book will consist of putting him in exactly that position and letting us identify with him as he faces the ultimate test.

Arc One

In Hero's Journey terms, this is the ordinary world the hero lives in before the big change that catapults him into the special world of challenge and fear, suspicion and skill mastery, tests and tasks, allies and enemies. We meet our protagonist and his world, the family, friends, lovers he thinks he can count on as allies. We learn his weaknesses, the inner need that this ordeal will resolve by testing him to the limit.

We need the ordinary world so that the special world will be special enough. We need a glimpse of Clarice Starling's ordinary life as an FBI trainee before we see her in Hannibal Lecter's very special world.

Accepting the Adventure

Just as amateur detectives in a mystery novel must commit to solving the crime, so must suspense heroes accept the adventure. Often, they are reluctant heroes, who don't want to leave their ordinary worlds to head into danger (and who can blame them?). Something must force them to act, something must be so important that they throw caution to the winds.

In *Hostage*, Talley's ordinary world is his new life as a cop in a boring suburb where nothing ever happens, which is just how Talley likes it. The special world is the world of hostage negotiation, which he hoped he'd left behind and would do anything not to be forced back into.

Chapter one begins with a robbery in which a convenience store owner is shot and lies bleeding, perhaps dead. This is bad enough from Talley's point of view, since he wants a quiet life.

So what happens next? What *has to* happen next?

Things get worse.

How?

The robbers decide to drive to Mexico and hole up until the robbery case blows over. Great plan, except for one little thing. Their cheap pickup truck dies an ignominious death on a side road leading to the freeway.

Okay, they think, we'll steal a car. And they just happen to have stalled right near an affluent housing development, so there are plenty of high-quality cars to choose from. We're on page 18 now, and we're getting closer to the hostage situation. (One more function of the prologue, not to mention the title, is that we're already thinking *hostage* before the robbers do.) All they want at this point is another getaway vehicle, but we're expecting them to take hostages and we want to know the people who will become their captives.

Which is precisely when we meet sixteen-year-old Jennifer Smith and her ten-year-old brother, Thomas. As might be expected from their respective ages, Jennifer resents having to take care of her younger brother, and he's giving her a hard time. Typical kid stuff—until it's interrupted by the robbers, who take the kids into Daddy's study. Daddy's response to the situation is more than a little odd. When the robbers demand the keys to his car, he says, "That's what you want, the car?" almost as if he were expecting them to demand something else. He readily agrees to turn over the car and then—

Things get worse.

How?

The doorbell rings. It's a cop. In uniform.

The robbers shoot him, but he's able to radio his base before dying on the doorstep.

It's only page 26. See what I mean about suspense on every page?

What created that suspense?

First, Crais started small, with the convenience store heist, and escalated *at every possible turn.* This resulted in two shootings in the first twenty-six pages, which adds to our suspense through the rest of the book by showing us that these guys aren't afraid to spill blood. When they threaten to kill the children, we believe them.

Second, Crais added complications and obstacles at exactly the right places. Whenever something could go wrong, it did go wrong. Bad luck is compounded by more bad luck, which "forces" the bad guys to do more bad things to save themselves. There isn't a moment of rest for them—or for the reader.

The Four Outcomes

A character wants something, something concrete in the here-and-now. Will he get it? There are four possible outcomes: "Yes," " No," "No, and furthermore," and "Yes, but." The first two outcomes *do absolutely nothing to move the plot.*

Think of the Jimmy Stewart character, George Bailey, in *It's A Wonderful Life.* Thanks to his absent-minded uncle, he's lost a huge sum of money belonging to the investors in his savings and loan company. So he goes to the richest man in town, played by Lionel Barrymore, and asks for the money he needs.

Barrymore could say yes: "Sure, for an old friend like you, anything." Jimmy gets the money, his uncle stays out of the loony bin, his investors are repaid, and writer-director Frank Capra makes the shortest movie in Hollywood history. Jimmy never jumps off the bridge, never meets Clarence the angel, and the audience is cheated of the catharsis we bought our tickets to experience.

Or Lionel, the meanest man in town, says, "No." Just no. Nothing else. It doesn't help Jimmy, but the trouble is, it doesn't hurt him either. Think about it. If Lionel just says, "No," nothing more, then Jimmy hasn't lost anything by asking. He's no worse off than he was when he went in the door—which means the writer has wasted our time in presenting the scene. It doesn't move the story because it doesn't change the hero's essential position.

Which is why Capra has Lionel give a different answer. A simple "no" isn't mean enough for the meanest man in town. Instead, Capra has Barrymore say, "No, I won't give you the money, *and furthermore*, I'm going to personally see to it that you get sent to jail for fraud and your dotty uncle goes to the funny farm." *I'll get you, my pretty, and your little dog, too.*

Now we have movement. We've taken our hero from frying pan to fire; he's worse off than he would have been had he stayed home and tried to deal with the losses on his own. Capra has pushed George Bailey to the point where it seems right for him to stand on that bridge and jump in.

The "no, and furthermore" answer is one of the two outcomes that will move the story and fill the middle of your suspense novel with ever-deepening complications. Whatever your characters do in the middle of the book should not only fail, it should fail in such a way that it makes their situations actively worse than they were before.

Put enough "no, and furthermore" outcomes in your novel, and you'll soon have a nice thick middle, as your hero struggles to extricate herself from the fire and get back into that nice, safe frying pan.

What about the "yes, but"? This outcome presents interesting possibilities. What if Lionel had said to Jimmy: "Sure you can have the money, boy. I'll just take your soul in return." Now our hero must decide what's more important to him; if he takes Lionel up on his offer, the rest of the story will deal with the consequences of selling his soul and his belated realization that it wasn't such a good deal. There have been more than a few operas constructed on the "yes, but" outcome, and, when you come to think about it, all the "yes, but" outcomes involve the soul in one way or another.

The most interesting use of the "yes, but" outcome is the "yes" with a hidden "but." Our hero gladly accepts the "yes" part of the answer, and settles down in the comfortable belief that he's being helped. And then, when he least expects it, the hidden "but" pops up—and the hero is plunged into distrust and danger once again.

The Four Outcomes in Hostage

Three guys go to rob a convenience store. Do they get away with the money? *Yes, but* they shot the owner, which means the stakes are higher than they'd planned.

They decide to escape to Mexico. Do they make it? *No, and furthermore* their car breaks down and they go in search of one to steal.

Do they get that second car and make their getaway? *No, and furthermore* they take hostages and kill a cop. At every turn, they dig themselves in deeper and deeper, which means they must take more and more drastic action that will keep the plot boiling.

Yes, but the robbers aren't the heroes. How do the Four Outcomes affect Jeff Talley?

After losing the hostage in the prologue, all Talley wants is a quiet life without major responsibility. Does he get it?

No, and furthermore, a store owner and one of his own cops are shot, *and furthermore,* he's about to be dragged back into a hostage negotiation situation, *and furthermore—*

This is only chapter one. The stakes will ratchet up throughout the book, and the mechanism by which they ratchet is the Four Outcomes scenario.

And if you think that's the end of the "yes, but" and "no, and furthermore" outcomes in this book, you'll soon find out that *every scene in the book ends with one of the two plot-moving outcomes.* Even the ones that look like simple *noes* and *yesses* will turn out to have hidden *buts* and *furthermores* lurking inside.

Suspense Writing

One more reason why this story moves so quickly: the pace of the writing.

What does that mean?

It means, first and foremost, that the prose is spare. Crais gives us just exactly as much information as we need to understand this moment in time and nothing more. There are no "extras" here, no long descriptive passages or internal monologues. We do go inside people's heads from time to time, but for the most part, they think about what's happening *now*, not what happened in the past. To the extent that the past enters into their thoughts, it's for a few short paragraphs and it's directly related to something happening in the present.

One decision is quickly followed by consequences that lead to a second decision, new consequences, a third decision, etc. There isn't much time for contemplation between events; one event happens right on top of another like a twenty-car pile-up on the Santa Ana Freeway.

The dialogue is crisp, which means that people say exactly what they think in no more words than it takes to get the idea across. Everyone is businesslike, speaking to the point, which fits because there is much at stake and no time for small talk.

Paragraphs are short, sentences shorter. All these devices working together create a sense of urgency.

We have our hostage situation and our reluctant hostage negotiator. So what could make things worse at this point?

- The robbers discover that the house is equipped with a lot of cameras and monitors, which allow them to see what the cops are doing outside.

- Then they find the money. Lots and lots of money. We're on page 57; still well inside Arc One, and our plot has thickened into cement. They don't make any decisions about the money yet, but we readers have a pretty strong sense that this information changes things in ways we have yet to understand.

- Ten-year-old Thomas manages to whisper to his sister on page 60, "I know where Daddy has a gun." This is our first hint that the internal dynamics of the hostage crisis won't be Bambi vs. Godzilla after all; it seems Bambi has a trick up his sleeve.

- We meet a mobster named Sonny Benza and learn that Thomas's daddy is his accountant. All of Benza's financial records are in the house, which is pretty serious because Benza is a big-time crook whose records could send a lot of people, including him, to jail.

- He doesn't want to go to jail.

Benza's records are in Smith's house and Smith's house is surrounded by cops. Once the hostage situation is resolved, cops will swarm all over that house and Sonny's enterprises will see the unwelcome light of day. Benza can see only one solution: to "own" the cop in charge of the case.

That's Talley. And that's the end of Part One. It's also Plot Point One and the end of Arc One. Let's look at the escalation process. We go from robbery to shooting to hostage taking to cop killing in very short order, and then we switch gears from the hostage situation to organized crime trying to cover itself by targeting Talley.

He thinks his biggest problem is holding on until other cops arrive to take over the hostage negotiation. *We know* his biggest problem is whatever Benza is going to do to "own" him. That's why suspense rests on the reader being two steps ahead of the character. We anticipate the trouble Talley doesn't even know is out there, and it heightens our emotional response to everything he does.

Alfred Hitchcock's famous story about the bomb under the table is relevant here. The great director said that the way to create suspense is to show a bomb under a card table and then show four men playing cards. The game could be the dullest thing imaginable, the dialogue could be flat, the scenery boring, but the audience is on the edge of their seats because they know what the card players don't: *there's a bomb under the table.* Every time someone shifts in his seat or gets up from the table, the audience wants to shout: *"Get out of there!"*

By showing Benza making plans to "own" Talley, Crais has let the audience know there's a bomb under our hero.

He detonates it in Arc Two.

Arc Two

P.G. Wodehouse, who in addition to his wonderful Jeeves books wrote musical comedies in the twenties, gave the following advice about what to do in the middle of your story. "Never," Sir Pelham advised, "let anyone sit down in the second act."

And if you think of a classic farce—whether it's a play by Molière, a Bertie Wooster/Jeeves novel, or a Marx Brothers movie—you see at once how effective that advice is. Doors open and skimpily dressed blondes pop out just when the gimlet-eyed aunt is visiting. The maid is found in the closet with the constable from the village. The pompous banker mistakenly believes the chorus girl is an heiress and treats her accordingly—and then mistakes the real heiress for a gold-digging chorus girl. Complications are set in motion that will cause the second-act curtain to come down on a scene of hilarious confusion.

Think of suspense as farce without the laughs. Something must be happening to your hero at all times; even moments of seeming safety must be fraught with possible danger. Will the peace last? Can this old friend be trusted? Will the police act, or have they been corrupted by the evil opponent? Can we cross the border into Poland or will the customs officials spot our phony passports?

The Pendulum

The middle of a suspense novel is a swinging pendulum of emotion. The hero veers wildly between trust and distrust, safety and danger. In the classic movie *Suspicion*, the wife alternates between blind trust in her husband and suspicion that he married her for money. The pendulum swings against the husband when she learns things that lead her to believe he is trying to kill her. He continually assures her of his love, but every time she relaxes into a normal, loving relationship, something else happens to rouse her suspicion.

The middle of a fairy tale involves tasks and tests the hero must perform in order to win the princess. The tasks increase in danger and difficulty until finally the hero emerges triumphant over his older, stronger brothers. The same pattern exists in the suspense novel; the hero practices for the final confrontation by overcoming challenges from lesser opponents or by escaping from imprisonment. In some cases, the hero fails the early tests and appears to be on the verge of failing the final test as well. A certain amount of trial and error makes an interesting middlebook as your hero learns the skills he will need to confront the opponent in the end. And of course, a hero who has failed once or even twice creates a great deal of suspense as he goes for the third try. (Note the magic number three, a powerful number in fairy tales.)

Isolate Your Hero

One of the tests a suspense hero must deal with is the increasing isolation from his or her usual support system. This is a vital element in a good suspense novel. Your hero can't go to the police; they don't believe him when he complains he's being followed by a man who is never there when they come around to check on his complaint. Your hero's friends and lovers tell her she has to "get over it" and refuse to believe that she's been threatened by a man no one else has ever seen. The hero's isolation may begin earlier, but it is deepened to the point where she is wholly alone in the middlebook. One by one, her supports fail her. One by one, the social structures she has always depended on disappear or turn actively hostile.

Why?

Think about it. First, our hero needs to grow up, to make a transition from one stage of life to another. She must be forced to fall back on her own inner resources when facing the ultimate challenge. If she has too much help, we won't believe in the transformation. Second, our hero is on a quest for the elixir, and we won't think she's earned it if she hasn't gone through hell. If she has too much help and support, it's not hell, it's purgatory at best; and that just doesn't cut it, elixir-wise.

The most important reason to strip away all your hero's old supports: if all the characters inside the book are lost to her, who's left?

Clap if you believe in fairies.

That's the ultimate reason why our hero must face these tests alone: because the one person left who believes in her isn't in the book at all. It's the reader, and the close identification with the hero you want your reader to feel can only come about if the hero is truly alone. Surround your hero with friends and you lose the intense identification that makes true suspense so compelling.

Dick Francis does this to perfection in *Nerve*. The premise of the book is that a young jockey, Rob Finn, is suspected of losing his nerve— and as a result, losing races. The first time he loses a race, he is publicly scolded by the horse's owner. As his luck worsens, the rumor that he's lost his nerve flies around the track. Other jockeys avoid him, and bettors and owners castigate him. Finally, he loses the confidence of the owner he's been riding for; his dream of being a winning jockey seems all but over. As if that weren't enough, he is called a coward by a television commentator and his failure is gloated over by his enemies.

Hitting Bottom

But Francis isn't finished taking his hero down the path to hell, because the real hell isn't what other people, however influential and important to Rob emotionally, think of him. Rob hits bottom the day he looks in the mirror and questions himself: Are they right? Have I really lost my nerve?

The isolation brought about by others turning on him leads to that moment, for if Rob had the confidence of even one friend, he might never stand before that mirror. And for us, the readers, to have the full experience of hitting bottom, of facing our inner demons, we need to be alone with Rob.

Rob decides that, no, he has not lost his nerve. He is the same rider he always was—which means that his trouble comes from without and has been engineered by someone else. He makes a conscious decision to find out who that person is and pay him back. This is the turning point of the novel—and it happens in the middle of the book.

Rift Within the Team

Stories that involve confrontations between two organized groups use Rift Within the Team as a middlebook suspense generator. Each team has an overarching goal: win the murder case, for example. The prosecution wants to convict, the defense to prove innocence. The district attorney answers to supervisors who may have very different ideas on how to conduct the case, creating Rifts Within the Prosecution Team. The defense lawyer may have an assistant who's really selling him out to the D.A. or a witness who's accepted a bribe to change her testimony. Rifts Within the Team allow conflict, suspense, mini-arcs, and mini-goals to take place before the big confrontation between the two teams.

One example of Rift Within the Two Teams can be found in Tom Clancy's *The Hunt for Red October.* There are two major focal points: Red Sub and U.S. Sub. They are in potential conflict, and *inside each sub* there is internal conflict. The Red Sub conflict is that its captain wants to defect to the U.S. and some of his men aren't in sympathy with that aim. The U.S. Sub conflict is that its captain believes the Red Sub captain and wants to help him defect, while most of his men think the Red Sub is out to destroy them.

Red Sub answers to Moscow; U.S. Sub to Washington, D.C., creating two lesser focal points. In Moscow and in D.C. there are internal conflicts as well. Four focal points = four places for internal conflict, and that's *on top of* the essential to-the-death conflict *between* the Reds and the U.S. forces.

Rift Within the Team keeps suspense high even when the two major forces aren't in direct conflict with one another. Because, let's face it, once the two major forces are in direct conflict with one another, we're at the end of the story. Someone will win, someone will lose, and it's over. You can't let that happen in chapter nine, so you delay the major conflict and play out a bunch of smaller, but still exciting, conflicts within each team. The key is that *these internal conflicts must relate directly to the overall conflict.*

How does Rift Within the Team occur in Robert Crais's *Hostage?*

The sheriff's department leader, Martin, moves too fast, sending cops into the perimeter (remember, the robbers can see it all on the security system monitors). The robbers freak out and threaten to burn down the house. Talley and Martin exchange heated words, and Talley has to stick around to save the deteriorating situation. He's dragged back into hostage negotiating in spite of himself.

Rift Within the Team creates slippage. A not-bad status quo, such as the one Talley reached with the hostage takers, can move backwards into something worse, which then gives our hero the chance to reclaim the former status quo as a victory without the writer having to ratchet things further.

What am I talking about?

We've had threats to the kids. We've had a murdered cop. We've had a near-fatal attack on Daddy. What can Crais do to top this?

Well, he could have one of the robbers kill or injure one of the kids.

But he doesn't want to. He needs Thomas to be able to move through those crawl spaces and find that cell phone, and he's got bigger plans for Jennifer later in the book.

So instead he sends in the cops, creating a moment of terror that the robbers will find Thomas out of bed (he's gone to look for Daddy's gun), and then resolves the situation by putting things back pretty much the way they were before. It's a lateral move, yet our hearts pound while Thomas creeps back to his room and our blood boils at the high-handed new cop. With any luck, we don't notice that *in the end nothing really changes* in the dynamic between cops and hostage takers.

Raising the Stakes

Remember Sonny Benza and his dangerous tax records? Remember how he said he was going to "own" Talley?

We meet a man named Marion Clewes, and we get to watch him eat a fly. Leg by leg, wing by wing.

He's the guy Sonny sends to grab Talley's wife and daughter.

We know what Talley doesn't: that throughout the entire Rift Within the Team business, his wife and kid are headed for Nightmare City.

Talley learns about his family's kidnapping in chapter fourteen, when he's told that they will be killed if he doesn't retrieve two zip disks from Smith's house.

And, by the way, this is Midpoint, page 192 of a 373-page book.

The man who hoped never again to negotiate a hostage situation now faces two at once: the robbers inside the house, and *his own family in the hands of a psycho killer.*

Talk about "no, and furthermore."

Arc Three

The astute will realize that all of Arc Two was in fact setup for this moment, and yet as you read the book, you aren't wondering when something exciting is going to happen, because it's already happening. By using mini-goals, mini-arcs, rifts within the team, lateral action, and the four outcomes, Crais has kept us on the edge of our seats while we waited for the bomb to go off.

Arc Three is where the hero becomes proactive. He's been reacting to whatever the villain's been throwing at him (like Dick Francis's hero in *Nerve*), and now he's hit bottom, faced the worst that could happen (at least in his own mind), and now he's going to bring it home to the bad guy. He's not going to sit around being made a victim any longer; he's arming himself and going into the lion's den.

That's one template for Arc Three. It's a very common one, and it works if Arc Two was a passive, taking-it-on-the chin arc. That's what happens in a number of stalking-oriented tales because it takes a while for the ordinary person to accept that she's being stalked, that what's happening to her is on purpose and not just random urban weirdness. This process is helped along by all those friends and allies who keep telling her, "It's just kids, honey," or "It's all in your head." The police, too, blow her off, telling her there's nothing she can do and refusing to believe that charming ex-boyfriend is really a vicious killer. Even the heroine's husband tells her she "needs to get away for a while," humoring instead of believing her.

So when she finally accepts the reality of the stalking and the fact that she's in this alone, that's when she can become the hero by turning the tables and going after the villain.

Other suspense novels put the Midpoint action of hitting bottom at Plot Point Two. In these stories, the hero may go proactive earlier, only he fails, usually spectacularly. He may fail because his heart wasn't pure, or because he's missing a crucial piece of information, or because he's after the wrong goal. That failure brings him to the hitting-bottom stage, and the experience renews him, teaches him the right goal, or gives the hidden piece of information he needs to make it all work.

In *Hostage*, Arc Three finds Talley back in charge of the hostage situation and so desperate to resolve it that he pushes too hard. He uses his superb negotiating skills to get the injured Smith out of the house, but his motive isn't to save the Smith children, but his own wife and child. He's so single-minded that he actually assaults Smith inside the ambulance, trying to bring the man to consciousness so he can be questioned.

Smith's trip to the hospital changes everything for Benza as well. Now Benza not only has to retrieve the disks with his information on them, he has to silence Smith before he starts talking. This gives Crais two places to focus our attention: the home where the hostage drama is being enacted, and the hospital where Smith lies vulnerable and unprotected. Splitting the Team is another middlebook ploy in the suspense novel; by doubling the locations where events happen, the writer can double the number of suspenseful moments.

Marion Clewes the fly-eater makes an attempt to kill Smith in the hospital. Talley saves Smith's life, then tells Smith that Benza has his own wife and daughter. He begs for help, but Smith refuses to talk.

Benza's henchman calls with a new, improved plan. His people will show up at the Smith house pretending to be FBI and Talley will let them take over and go into the house first so they can get the disks.

We're coming into the home stretch (page 278, about 100 to go) and the players are all gathering in one place for the showdown.

Inside the house, Thomas finds Daddy's gun.

We're on page 312. A ten-year-old with a gun faces down a huge psycho killer (don't even ask) who's armed with a knife.

What could make this worse?

Thomas pulls the trigger.

Click!

No bullets.

The kids race upstairs to the reinforced safe room.

The psycho killer sprinkles gasoline all over and lights a match.

Talley faces off against the phony FBI guys, who would just as soon let the house burn. He knows he's risking his family's lives if he tries to save the Smith children, and he also knows it's his moral and legal duty to save them.

He does his duty.

Building to Climax

The astute will once again realize that important as saving the Smith children may be, it's not the main event. Everything in Arcs Two and Three simply cleared away the underbrush so we could concentrate on the real confrontation, the one between Talley and Benza, with Talley's wife and child as the bait and the prize. Similar things happen in mysteries as the detective clears up mini-puzzles, exposes lies, and tracks down red herrings before coming at last to the big solution that solves the murder.

Crais built to this climax by ratcheting up the stakes at every turn. Now his Daniel is about to go into the lion's den. His hero is facing the hostage negotiation of his life. Can he do it? Can the man we saw in the prologue rise to the ultimate occasion and save his own child from death at the hands of a cruel sadist?

Ending chapters with a cliffhanger is another powerful suspense tool.

8. Endings Are Hard, II

Satisfying the Suspense Reader

ENDINGS ARE HARD. How many times have you waded through pages upon pages of heated prose, your pulse racing and your fingers flipping the pages like mad, only to be disappointed by the so-called "big finish"? How many times have you put down a book with a sigh, thinking, "If only the ending had lived up to that thrilling opening chapter" or "What a great premise for a novel—too bad this writer couldn't deliver." When your friends ask how you liked the book you say, "It was great, but the ending fell flat."

Why? What happened? How did a writer who had you with him all the way drop the ball in the final ten yards?

For one thing, writers are only human. As the book nears its close, they get tired. Eager to finish—and not incidentally, to pick up the next installment of their advance—they may rush through scenes they ought to linger over. Piling one sensational event upon another is not the key to a great ending; it's a recipe for creating a dissatisfied reader. Racing against a ticking clock is what the hero of your book needs to do, not what you the writer ought to be doing.

The second problem is also time-related: writers often revise the earlier chapters as they go along, not just correcting grammar and spelling, but delving more deeply into the characters, adding telling details to the setting, building more suspense. Then when they come to the ending, all of a sudden they realize their book is *due* and there isn't any time for revision. The closing chapters can feel like a first draft instead of a finished product because the author hasn't taken the time to go back through those chapters and give them the full treatment.

How to Finish Your Book Before It Finishes You _____

The obvious answer to these problems is to make sure you have sufficient time to do your ending right. The trouble is—that's easy to say, harder to do. Here are a few tricks and strategies to help you make sure you'll have the time and energy to give your slam-bang ending its true value.

And the Last Shall Be First

One radical thought: write the last chapter first.

Well, okay, not exactly the last chapter and not exactly first, but the truth is, you know pretty early on who your ultimate villain is and you know your hero must confront that ultimate villain sometime, some-where. So pick the most dramatic setting you can think of, put your hero and villain in that spot, and let them duke it out. Do this fairly early in your writing process, when you still have a full head of steam and lots of time to revise. Then set that scene aside and go back to the linear story.

If you're working the four arcs, go back to your confrontation scene whenever you reach a plot point and look at it again. See if you've learned anything in the writing of that arc that would add resonance to the con-frontation. Did you discover that the villain was a crack shot? If so, how about making your hero a moving target and letting the villain take pot-shots at her? Did you decide the villain's wife was almost as evil as he is? If so, she'd make a fine first-enemy confrontation before your hero gets to the final showdown with the ultimate villain. Perhaps your original scene took place on a rocky cliff, but you just finished a scene on the villain's yacht—you might rewrite your scene and have it take place on the yacht (in a perfect storm at sea, of course).

Use the Setting

Each time you revisit the confrontation scenes, ask yourself if you're get-ting the most out of your characters, your situations, and your setting. Maybe it's the underground aspect, but one book that comes to mind when I think of great settings exploited to the max is Nevada Barr's *Blind Descent*. Our hero, park ranger Anna Pigeon, is claustrophobic. She's also assigned to a national park whose most famous asset is a cave. Already we have an interesting situation, and the first time Anna descends into the cave is a memorable exercise in scene setting. Because Anna is hypersensitive to the idea of being underground, she notices every detail that could possibly give rise to fear, and as a result, we the readers feel her emotional resistance to the place.

That's the setup. We've been inside the cave, we know what it's like, and we know how much Anna hates and fears the place. So when Arc Four rolls along and Anna gets trapped in the cave with an armed killer, we're primed for an adrenaline rush of action and suspense. And we get exactly that. It's dark—which means both that Anna can't see the killer and that she can't always be seen. The darkness is both advantage and peril, and Barr uses it as both. The killer has a gun, but the killer can't see to aim it.

There are twists and turns and odd rock formations, places to hide, curved paths that distort the sound so that you can't tell where someone else is. Someone in the cave is injured—does Anna stay with her, leave her there and go for help, or abandon her? Meanwhile, it's cold and water trickles down the rocks, making them slippery to hold onto and walk on.

Barr milks that cave for all it's worth. She gets suspense mileage out of every nook and cranny, every stalagmite and stalactite, and that's what I'm talking about when I urge you to do the same with your chosen stand-off setting. Ask yourself these questions:

- What is there in the setting that could be used as a weapon, either by the villain or the hero?

- How can the setting be made even more dangerous to the hero?

- Is the setting remote, so that outside help is unlikely?

- Are there natural dangers that threaten the hero as much as anything the villain could do?

- Does the setting have any other meaning in the story that takes on an ironic edge now that it's become a place of confrontation and danger?

- Can the setting be made even more frightening by, say, turning out the lights, or cutting off the oxygen?

You'll also notice that Barr gives the final-confrontation-in-the-cave situation three chapters from descent to ascent. That's about right for a really well-developed climax, and you'll also note that there are mini-goals and mini-arcs within those three chapters.

Use the Characters

We need to see the villain pulling out all the stops. The Wicked Witch of the West is as wicked as they come, and she pulls no punches in her confrontation with little Dorothy. We've been waiting for this conflict, and we aren't going to be satisfied if the Big Bad Villain melts too quickly. Whatever powers the writer gave the villain need to be put into play at the end, nothing held back. He's fighting for his very life, and he has no scruples about doing whatever it takes to win.

But our hero by this time isn't powerless. Whatever she learned in the middlebook comes into play now. All the new skills she's mastered plus whatever strengths she started with need to be used. Any allies she made among the enemy ranks need to turn their coats now, and we need to believe in their transformation.

Secondary characters make good interim targets. Good-guy allies die for the cause; bad-guy allies take a bullet for the chief. Turncoats pay the price. And all of this takes time. From Plot Point Two to the final *mano-a-mano* can take two to three chapters, and probably should. Don't run through the foreplay too quickly; we readers have waited a long time for this, and we're ready to enjoy the whole thing, nothing skipped over.

Read John Le Carré's *The Night Manager* and see how he develops the Big Bad Guy character, showing his ruthlessness, his cleverness, his love for his young son, his possessive affection for his girlfriend, his egotistical power tripping—every single aspect of this man's character becomes something our hero will either suffer because of or learn to exploit as a weakness. Every secondary character also has a role to play for good or ill; they either thwart the hero or help him, and sometimes they do both unwittingly.

When the climax arrives and our hero seems to be in an impossible predicament, the B team steps in. This consists of the spymasters back in London, who are fighting their own bureaucratic war within the intelligence establishment. Every move they make is likewise rooted in character development that Le Carré put in motion at the beginning of the story. Clues planted in Arc One about who these men are under stress bear fruit in Arc Four. Even when it seems that tables are turning, we believe because we've seen enough aspects and facets of character to make the twists and reversals credible.

A Full Measure of Justice

The payoff has to be worthy of the setup. If you've shown your readers blow-by-blow pictures of the suffering victims, your readers will not be satisfied if the serial killer is marched away in handcuffs at the end of the book. We want—we *need*—to see him suffer and perhaps die in order to experience catharsis. Even his death cannot truly balance the suffering we saw him cause, but if he suffers nothing, we are left unsatisfied. A writer who has given us less detail about the suffering victims might get away with a less powerful ending, but if the balance is off, we feel the ending has not been worthy of the rest of the book.

In a similar vein, the villain has to be worthy of the hero's effort. The villain your hero confronts must be worthy of her ultimate efforts; he must be bigger than life and twice as dangerous. He must be *shown* to be dangerous, in that he wants your hero's total destruction and has the apparent means to get what he wants. The murderer in a whodunit may turn out to be a pathetic loser awakening our pity; the suspense villain had better remain a powerful force for evil if your hero's struggle is to have meaning. Jack the Giant Killer needs a giant. Snow White needs a jealous queen; a mere neurotic stepmother with a narcissistic personality disorder won't do.

The battle itself must likewise be worthy. In a suspense novel, the confrontation between hero and villain is the climax—it must last long enough and be told in sufficient detail to satisfy the reader, and it must involve ingenuity and skill as well as sheer physical strength. We need to see the hero try and fail, try and fail again, then try and succeed—only to be confronted by another, stronger enemy or strategy. When this doesn't happen, we feel unsatisfied.

An easy, time-honored way to add suspense is to cross-cut between scenes involving the hero in peril and other scenes. It's the old "meanwhile, back at the ranch" ploy; you lock the hero in a room with the time bomb ticking away, then cut to an unrelated scene. We read the second scene as quickly as possible; we can't wait to get back to the locked room and find out how our hero is doing. He tries to loosen his bonds; he fails.

Cut to the villain, on his way to commit whatever villainous acts are on his mind. He succeeds.

Back to the locked room. Hero tries again; hero fails again. The time bomb is ticking.

Read Mary Higgins Clark's *A Stranger Is Watching* to see how it's done. Our heroine is tied to a ticking bomb underneath Grand Central Station, in a hidden place only the homeless know. As if that weren't enough tension, there's a small child with her, and if she can't untie the two of them and go for help, not only will they die, they'll take hundreds of innocent people waiting for trains upstairs with them.

While the clock ticks, Clark shows every movement of every muscle as our heroine strains against her bonds. We feel every trickle of sweat down her face, every rush of blood to her heart as she thinks about the consequences. The time ticks away, not just in the story, but in Clark's prose; on every page, she reminds us exactly how few seconds are left. Clark keeps us tied to this painful situation for exactly the same amount of time that our heroine is tied to the bomb, so that we're reading in real time, not speeding it up for the sake of getting to the climax.

Endings that Satisfy

Action without feeling—great for a Bruce Willis movie, deadly for a suspense novel.

The more emotion you can pack into your final scenes, the more you will create readers who don't just like your books, they *love* your books and they can't wait to tell their friends all about the new writer they've discovered.

Think I'm just being a chick here?

Perhaps you think that what I mean by emotion-packed is people crying all over the place. No—what I mean by emotion is resonance, resolution, a sense of destiny fulfilled, of a human being living to his highest potential and reaping well-earned rewards.

Remember how you felt when Dumbledore awarded those points to Gryffindor in *Harry Potter and the Sorcerer's Stone*? Remember how thrilled you were when Princess Leia, Luke Skywalker, and Han Solo were honored at the end of the first *Star Wars*? How about Dr. Richard Kimball knowing he's finally proved his innocence at the close of *The Fugitive*?

The more the resolution of the situation matters to the hero, the more it matters to the reader. At the end of *Blind Descent*, Anna Pigeon hasn't just unmasked a murderer, she's faced her own deepest fear and come out stronger. At the end of Jeffery Deaver's *A Maiden's Grave*, a world-weary, cynical hostage negotiator has a chance to renew his faith in humanity with a young deaf teacher, and the teacher has proved her own bravery to herself. The ordeal has not only succeeded in saving children's lives but in giving each of them a new life to look forward to.

You don't get an ending like that without a lot of setting up. We can't know how much a new love would mean to the old jaded cop unless we trace his past experiences with his now-dead wife (and we do this in Arc Two, don't we?). We can't feel the strength of the young teacher's connection to this man she can only see through an upstairs window without being inside her head and realizing how lonely she's been since she lost her hearing. That setup is for nothing unless the writer gives us the full payoff, bringing these two people together at the end in a way that shows us they have a chance for happiness together.

T. Jefferson Parker's *Little Saigon* brings his hero fully into the bosom of his family. The younger son, the outsider, the despised one, the boy who feels inferior to his big brother and responsible for the drowning death of his little sister, is now, at last, a completely acknowledged son of his powerful father. Where did his journey start? At a table in a Vietnamese nightclub where he felt acutely his brother's legendary status and his own marginal acceptance. Where does it end? At the family table, where his father tells him he is loved and respected.

Endings that Let the Reader Down

These are some of the good endings. What are the ending-killers you need to watch out for? On my all-time top ten list:

1. The contrived, Hollywood-style ending that depends upon a complete character transplant. The villain suddenly turns into Little Mary Sunshine; the hero who hasn't been through the fire suddenly becomes Superman.

2. The big secret finally revealed that turns out to be not so big, and for the reader with any level of sophistication, not so secret.

(N.B.: Everyone knows some children are sexually abused. It ain't a big secret anymore, and it's too sad to become a cliché.)

3. The ending that depends upon information withheld from the reader until the last minute when that information really should have been delivered earlier.

4. The missed opportunity ending, in which the author stubbornly refuses to put the real action on the page and instead does an "I just heard on the radio that Mr. Big is dead" thing.

5. The violence-for-its-own-sake ending, in which seven people we didn't care much about in the first place are gunned down just to prove how bad the bad guy is. Prove it in Arcs Two and Three; that's what setup is for.

6. The double ending that depends upon our believing the villain is dead, only to have him pop up again in a totally unbelievable way.

7. The ending that depends upon a quick and "sweet" resolution of conflicts that are really too complex and thorny for easy solutions.

8. Insufficient justice.

9. Insufficient setup for the payoff.

10. The outline-for-an-ending that goes through the motions without sufficient depth or detail. The ending that screams, "I was on deadline! What do you want from my life?"

Hostage: Arc Four

Talley and the phony FBI guys work together to breach the house, kill the robbers, and release the kids. (This is made a lot easier by a Rift Within the Enemy Team.) The bad guys start ripping up the office in search of the disks, which Talley knows Thomas has.

Final twist on Rift Within the Team: The Team Traitor.

Someone on our team was on the take from the beginning, working for Benza, and if that person had managed to get into the Smith house, Benza would have gotten his disks and—

And Talley's family would be safe. The Smiths might well have died, which would have been one more nightmare for Talley, but his wife and daughter would never have had to meet Marion Clewes.

So by acting the professional, Talley unknowingly put himself in the position of becoming Benza's target. He's paying the price for being a good hostage negotiator, and the price is that he has to become an even better one to save his own family.

The irony, the irony. Yes, this is irony, which has nothing at all to do with rain on your wedding day or cheap wisecracks by late-night comics.

And it's the ultimate Rift Within the Team: the Team Traitor, who must not be revealed until the last possible moment, and *whose every action prior to the betrayal must be re-examined and found to be consistent with that betrayal even though we didn't realize it at the time.*

Talley overcomes the Team Traitor and orders the arrests of the phony FBI guys. He goes to the hospital and takes the rescued Smith kids into their father's room. This time Smith agrees to cooperate with Talley by helping him get to Benza.

Mythic heroes often have to face the same challenge more than once. They fail the first test, as Sir Percival did when he's unable to heal the wounded Fisher King. Talley confronted Smith before and got nothing; this time, *because he put the Smith children's lives above everything else*, he has earned the right to Smith's help, just as Percival earned the right to heal the Fisher King on their second encounter.

Now Talley calls Benza's henchman and starts negotiating on behalf of his own wife and child. The cop who was afraid he could never successfully negotiate a hostage situation again is faced with the toughest negotiation of his life. And he can do it now, in chapters 26 and 27, because we've seen him resolve the Smith hostage crisis. He's been tested and tested and tested, and now he has his black belt and is up against the biggest negotiating challenge he (or we) can imagine.

That's what Arcs Two and Three are for: to get our champion ready for the Big Bout, the Long Program, the Super Bowl of his suspense life. Crais showed Talley overcoming one hair-trigger robber, one psycho-killer robber, phony FBI guys, a turncoat cop, and a closed-mouthed Mafia accountant to get to this place. When he faces the baddest of the bad, we sense it's an even match.

On page 345, Benza orders the murders of pretty much everyone in the book, from Talley to the FBI guys to Smith. This is how desperate the situation is; he's willing to wipe out his whole organization if he has to. Because if he doesn't, Mr. Really Big Bad Guy back east will whack him for being so careless as to let his records be exposed.

We're playing for all the marbles. And when it comes to thriller writing, anything less than all the marbles isn't worth playing for. Hold no marbles back.

The stand-off comes in stages. Talley confronts first one, then another henchman until he reaches Howell, the second in command. Then he tosses the guy one disk and says the guy can have the other after he sees his wife and child. He isn't, in the words of his opponent, "acting like a has-been cop who had been broken by the job and come to nowhereland to hide." (p. 353)

That was precisely what he was acting like in chapter two, if you recall. This is how far this experience has brought him, and we believe it because it's his enemy talking and *because we were there to witness his transformation.* This is the Hero's Journey come to life: Talley has gone from burned-out ordinary world to super-competence inside the special world of hostage negotiation, and now, having come through the fire, he faces the ultimate test.

Marion Clewes the fly-eater has a gun to Talley's wife's head. Talley has a gun to Howell's head. Howell has one disk; Talley has the other.

Who's going to blink first?

Whoever cares the most. And that's Talley.

So he drops his gun.

What? He just drops his gun and lets Howell have the disk?

What kind of heroic act is that?

Howell gets the disk and puts it into his laptop computer and we learn that it's *not* the second disk with Benza's information on it. It's blank.

Howell orders Clewes to kill everyone. Clewes raises his gun. He has his orders from Benza.

But instead of shooting Talley, Clewes shoots everyone else, including Howell. Which makes a weird kind of sense when you remember that Benza ordered the wipe-out of everyone who knew anything about the Smith situation because he's deathly afraid of Mr. Really Big Bad Guy back east finding out that he was so careless with his tax records.

The bad guys are on the run, only the Really Big Bad Guys won't let them run, so there is weeping and gnashing of teeth in the camp of the enemy, which is pretty much what there ought to be at the end of a good suspense novel.

Jeff Talley is no longer a burnout case. Hostage negotiations killed his soul, and now hostage negotiations have restored his soul and brought him back to his wife and daughter, who are no longer estranged from him because he has his soul back and he can show them his love. His nightmares about the blown case in the prologue are replaced by a daydream of forgiveness. He is now reconnected to life through the risking and saving of lives.

He has returned with the elixir.

Did he earn it? That's the key to the elixir thing; if we have a moment's hesitation in answering that question, we have a failed Hero's Journey. Earning is everything, and that's why Arcs Two and Three of a good thriller have to take us to hell and beyond. That's why Crais didn't let the Smith home be invaded by three stupid punks—instead, he gave us two stupid punks and a psychotic killer. That's why Crais didn't make Smith an ordinary accountant, but the accountant to the Mob. That's why Talley isn't just a former LAPD hostage negotiator who decided to move to the burbs; he's a burnout case who's barely hanging on by his fingernails.

Everything that could go to the max went to the max.

And that's what makes a thriller.

Sting in the Tail Endings

Just as the mystery has its tradition of "double" endings, so does the suspense genre. Some of these are two-tiered, like the two-solution mystery endings, and some just put a little sting in the tail to let us know it isn't entirely over.

The famous Hannibal Lecter line in *Silence of the Lambs* about "having an old friend for dinner" is one of those stinger endings. The ostensible Bad Guy, the serial killer known as Buffalo Bill, has been caught, but Lecter escaped from prison and is still at large. He calls Clarice Starling to gloat and remind her that he's still a menace to society. He's also promising to come back in a sequel, which isn't always the point of the stinger.

Often the stinger sets an ironic tone, telling the reader that while the hero has succeeded in one aspect of his quest, he's still got a long way to go. Other stinger endings, such as the ones in Jeffery Deaver's *A Maiden's Grave* and Michael Connelly's *The Poet*, add an extra layer to the story and bring in new dimensions.

Whether or not you use a sting in the tail ending has a lot to do with your overall worldview. The stinger is an ironic twist, a not-quite-happy ending that undercuts the traditional heroic victory over evil. So if you want that pure victory, go for all-out goodness at the end and leave out the stinger. Let everyone live happily ever after without a cloud of disillusion.

Me, I like clouds. Which is why Michael Connelly's *City of Bones* has my vote for Sting in the Tail of 2002.

What Can You Do for an Encore?

Not so long ago, I firmly believed that series suspense was impossible. Dick Francis, who introduced new protagonists with each title, felt the same. Once you'd taken your main character to hell and back, where could you go in a sequel that's worse than hell? How many times can one person confront a fate worse than death without the writer falling into a *Perils of Pauline* disaster-of-the-month trap?

Francis wrote his second book about a character he'd already used with *Whip Hand*. Sid Halley, first introduced in *Odds Against*, had lost his hand in an accident. *Odds Against* showed him coming to terms with his disability, and when the story finished, Francis said he had no plans for a second book about Halley.

Television producers thought otherwise. They saw a series in the character and they begged for a second adventure with him.

What do you do with a character who lost his hand and his career in book one and who in the same book started a second career and overcame his feelings of uselessness? Where could Francis go from there?

When a man has lost one hand, what's the worst thing that could happen to him?

Losing the other hand, of course.

And that's what Francis did: he put Sid Halley in a position where Very Bad Dudes threatened to destroy his good hand if he didn't play ball with them.

That's what an author trying for a meta-novel has to do: figure out where to take the character after the first resolution of his story. Yes, our detective has solved *this* crime, but has he learned more about his own identity? (That's Anne Perry's William Monk series, starring a Victorian police officer with amnesia. The meta-challenge for him is figuring out who he is—or who he used to be.)

Yes, Molly Cates saved *this* busload of children from fanatical kidnappers, but will she ever get to the truth about her father's death? (*Under the Beetle's Cellar*, and yes, Molly does find the truth in *All the Dead Lie Down*, the third book in the series. The questions about the death, however, began in the first book, Mary Willis Walker's *The Red Scream*.)

Or, thinking of the late great John D. MacDonald, how many of the hero's girlfriends can you kill off before readers refuse to invest their emotions in your stories?

In John D.'s case, it didn't seem to matter. Travis McGee met a new woman in every book, and if they didn't all die, a goodly number of them did, and Travis mourned for a while, but we readers were willing to follow him on his next outing just the same. One reason it didn't matter is that the books were action-adventure reads with mystery overtones. Travis McGee was a knight-errant, and knights always have fair ladies whom they don't marry and settle down with.

Dave Robicheaux, James Lee Burke's bayou detective, does get married and acquire a child, and that means that his emotional connections must be treated with more seriousness than McGee's. If one significant other dies, there must be mourning and regrouping before another can enter Robicheaux's life. Women and children are threatened in this series, but there's never a sense that they could be injured or killed without a devastating psychological impact on the hero.

Story arcs in this series involve Dave's first wife, his mourning for her and romance with a second woman, the growth and development of his adopted child. Each of these strands spans more than one book and each brings him closer to a family life, the loss of which would destroy him completely.

Burke takes us into the past as well, dealing in the eleventh book of the series *(Purple Cane Road)* with the death of Robicheaux's mother, which was mentioned in the first book, *The Neon Rain*. At the same time, Dave's daughter Alafair, named for his dead mother, is growing up and becomes a part of the story in a way she couldn't have done earlier. By waiting until book eleven to delve deeply into the mother's death, Burke adds another level to the resonance by involving the next generation.

The more you care, the more you have to lose. So one of the uses of the meta-novel is to show the character's deepening connections, his intense caring, for another person, someone who can't be replaced in the next book.

The death of significant others is becoming almost a standard plot point in the meta-novel. It's a way of taking the character to new depths and creating sympathy, while at the same time clearing the way for another relationship that will spark up a series in danger of sagging in the meta-middle. The death alone will not be enough to do this; the death must provoke change in the main character. The danger is that since the reader, presumably, already liked the main character, how can the author change her without losing what the readers liked?

As the meta-novel evolves, taking on some of the qualities of a long-running television drama series, it will be interesting to see how much suffering and loss readers can absorb without becoming saturated.

Part 3:
The Writing
Process

9. Scene and Style

The Basic Ingredients of the Novel

THE FOUR ARCS represent divisions of the Big Picture, and they make a great planning template and a wonderful revision tool. But a novel isn't *written* in the Big Picture, it's made up of a series of small pictures we call scenes.

What's the difference between a scene and a chapter?

Scenes are organic; chapters are artificial.

What Makes a Scene?

In the first place, scenes happen in real time. It's as if the reader is a fly on the wall, watching and listening as characters talk and move. We hear the characters speak in their own voices, we observe their body language, and we do it at the pace of real life, with no authorial summing-up tricks to make it go faster.

Second, scenes involve conflict. Not necessarily shove-a-gun-in-someone's-face conflict, but at the very least a sense of the characters being at odds in some way, out of sync, one wanting something the other can't or won't give.

Why conflict? Because two people agreeing about absolutely everything would be amazingly boring, would fail to move the story, and we readers would wonder why that scene was in the book at all.

Unless, of course, it's part of the setup. Oh, that's it, we think as we read about the happy couple. They're in total agreement *now*, but just wait—the big breakup is coming.

Because at bottom all stories are about change (or, in a very few cases, failure to change, which is in itself a form of change because opportunity is offered and declined, which means our protagonist doesn't just go back to where he was at the beginning, he's *worse off* because he could have changed but didn't.) That's the inexorable math of Story: no character can possibly come through Story unscathed. (See *The Remains of the Day* for wonderfully evocative proof of this fiction maxim.)

So if change is at the root of Story, how does it manifest itself in the small picture, the scene?

A Scene Driver Named Desire

Our protagonist wants something. If he's a detective, he wants to know whodunit. If she's a suspense heroine, she wants to go back to the peaceful life she had before some wacko started sending her dead flowers. If he's a spy, he wants to save the free world; if she's in a legal thriller she wants to get the Pelican Brief to the right people before the wrong people whack her.

Well, they can't get those things, can they? Not in Arc One, that's for sure.

So for scene purposes, they need to want something else, something lesser but still connected to the big goal, something that, ideally, pushes them harder into the plot point that climaxes whichever arc they're in.

This is vital. *Every single scene in the book must start from a position of wanting.*

"I want to have a good time at this party"—but it's going to be hard now that the host is dead on the floor. My amateur detective's nice simple want has turned into a situation that will force her to turn detective and start asking questions.

"I want to get the people who killed my girlfriend"—and in order to do that, I'll volunteer as a spy so I can go after Mr. Big Bad Guy, but right this minute my want is to pass all the tests so the spies will take me on as a recruit.

The small scene-level wants are like acorns from which spring giant oaks. They are the tiny pieces of colored glass that will, when put together, shine forth from the stained glass window of your plot.

Just as in the overarching plotline, just as in the arc, the scene contains a goal, a complication, tension, and resolution. At the end of *every scene in the book, bar none,* the protagonist must experience some change, for better or worse.

Worse is better. Change for the better, in the first three arcs, should turn into worse as soon as possible, or should contain the seeds of later getting worse-ness.

Why?

Because when things get worse, when the protagonist fails to get what he wants, he is forced to do something else. Something that propels him into more dangerous waters.

So every single scene must end with a "No, and furthermore"?

Not necessarily. Sometimes a "Yes, but" is more interesting than a straight No and sometimes a Yes brings a lot more headaches than a No would have done. It's all a matter of pushing the protagonist out of her comfort zone and into territory where she will be tested to the max.

But none of that can happen unless she wants something at the beginning of the scene—a scene goal that the reader understands from the outset. That's one of the beauties of the mystery form; we readily accept the detective's need to know as a perfectly clear, perfectly reasonable scene goal, and everything follows from that.

What does the suspense hero want as a scene goal?

To understand what's happening to him. To enlist official help in tracking down the bad guys. To have someone believe her. To get a passport or a ticket to Hong Kong or the key to the safety deposit box. To find that old photo album or grandfather's will, anything that will help unravel the tangled secrets of the past. To get Aunt Maisie out of her Alzheimer's fog just long enough to tell our heroine the truth about that long-ago phone call the night Daddy died.

It doesn't matter exactly what she wants so long as the reader understands what she wants and why she wants it and it relates in some way to the novel's big goal.

Surprises and Complications

If every single witness sits down with the detective and tells a straightforward narrative, no lies, no mistakes, no secrets, just a factual account of exactly what he knows and how he knows it, we'll have a short and intensely boring mystery novel.

If every suspense heroine sits down with Grandfather and receives a full, frank, open account of every single family secret, all the family skeletons, and the precise reason why Uncle Frank seems to want her dead, we'll have a short and intensely boring suspense novel.

In fact, we'll have a mystery novel without mystery and a suspense novel without suspense. Both genres depend rather heavily on secrets and lies, surprises and complications. And those must be introduced at the scene level.

When it comes to the big scenes, most writers get this. It's the small scenes that give us trouble. It's the scene where our detective sits over coffee with her best friend and bounces ideas about the murder around, only they both agree on absolutely everything and are really just committing exposition on one another. It's the scene where the spy gets his orders from MI5 and just stands there as we readers try to absorb a huge chunk of geopolitical backstory that is essential for our understanding of later events but bores us silly.

All scenes must involve some level of conflict and tension. All scenes must produce change.

The Night Manager, John Le Carré

Bureaucratic infighting among British intelligence agencies sounds like exactly the kind of dry, dull, arcane exposition I'm talking about. Who'd sit still to read page after page about what this cabinet officer said to that one at a Whitehall cocktail party?

Le Carré has us reading every word because:

- He puts human faces on every character he shows us (yes, even bureaucrats have faces).

- Every person represents a particular political viewpoint and has compelling personal reasons for fighting for that viewpoint.

- What's at stake is spelled out very clearly from the outset and is repeated in different ways at the start of every scene so we don't lose track of who stands for what.

- He shows us that bureaucratic infighting risks lives—most notably, the life of our hero, who's undercover and very vulnerable.

- The major players in this drama are in their own life-and-death struggle and there will be no survivors on the losing side.

- He creates a giant chess match between the forces of good and the forces of evil and sets up every move so that we know who's winning and who's losing at every single stage.

- Or at least we think we do. Once in a while the chess piece we thought was a lowly pawn gets queened and acquires more sinister power than we expected.

- The clashes among bureaucrats escalate along with the danger to our hero, so that we're racing toward two climaxes, not just one.

- As in any good team story, there are Rifts Within the Team in the bureaucratic storyline; there will be betrayals and traitors on both sides of the issue.

It's good to throw in a complete surprise every so often. That helpful police officer who turns out to be on the Big Bad Guy's payroll, that kind friend in *The Fugitive* who gives Dr. Kimball some money and then turns him in to the cops, that key to the bus station locker that contains a suitcase filled with money. Let the protagonist get a result he couldn't possibly have anticipated and see what he does with it.

How To Scene

Movie people use something called a storyboard, which actually shows pictures not unlike comic strips that indicate what the scenes will look like.

Writing storyboards is a way of putting down on paper some of the things you'll use in your finished scene. It helps focus the scene. The writer needs to know exactly what the character's scene goal is and convey that to the reader. Everything in the scene is subordinate to that goal, yet you'll need to put in things like physical description, interior monologue, all kinds of extras that can get lost if the writer's in too much of a hurry.

So you plan the scene beforehand, or you read the draft you've already written and look for places to go deeper, or things to cut because they don't move the goal. You ask yourself the journalism questions: who, what, where, when, why, and how.

Who are these people? How do they talk, what are they wearing, what are they doing as they talk? If they're walking along the beach, have you given the reader enough salt spray, smacking breeze, waves crashing on the beach, toes sinking into wet sand? How do they move their bodies? Does one talk with her hands? Is the other gazing out over the waves instead of looking at his companion?

Whose viewpoint is it? Are we inside the head of one character, or are we essentially watching both through a camera lens, unable to read any thoughts they don't express in some way?

Most important: how does this scene change things for one or both characters?

And what will he do next because of that change?

Action Produces Reaction

Once the scene has wrought change of some kind and degree, our character must react. Sometimes the reaction is swift and practically invisible to the naked eye. Other times the character stops and reflects upon the change, taking it in emotionally and intellectually before making a conscious decision about his next move.

Let's say our hard-boiled private eye talks to the nightclub singer about the murder of her saxophone-player boyfriend. He gets a lot of sarcasm and not much information, but he knows she's hiding something and she bites her lip and turns away when he mentions the Fat Man.

That's the scene. The sequel is that the detective reflects upon that behavior and comes to the conclusion that the Fat Man knows something.

So our detective goes into a bar, orders two shots of rye, and drops the whole case.

What?

No, of course, he doesn't. He drives his '56 Chevy to the Fat Man's penthouse apartment and tries to question him, only the Fat Man's hired goons rough him up and that's when he *knows* the Fat Man's up to his fat eyeballs in this case.

The reaction, the part where the character thinks about what happened at the end of the scene and absorbs its emotional impact, *must lead to a new scene.*

The new scene leads to another, and another, and pretty soon you've written a whole book.

Action produces reaction inside the scene as well. The detective's mention of the Fat Man caused the nightclub singer to look away and bite her lip, as though she wanted to say something but didn't dare. She reacted to the detective's action.

The detective's trip to the Fat Man brings out the goons who rough him up—a pretty strong reaction, and one that will cause the detective to suspect the Fat Man even more.

Fixing Problem Scenes

The first thing to look at when revising a scene is whether or not the viewpoint character has a clear scene goal. If not, that's the first thing to fix. If so, then what else could be wrong? A few scene problems and their solutions:

Talking Heads

Can we get those heads attached to actual bodies? Could those bodies move or at least twist their wedding bands or crack their knuckles or do something besides drink designer coffee? Props are a big help here; what can they hold in their hands? What physical action could they be doing as they talk?

Talking in a Vacuum

Dialogue is great. There's nothing better than letting your characters express themselves in their own voices. But you're writing a novel, not a screenplay, so those voices are attached to bodies and those bodies are in a physical location. Show me. Take me there. Take all five senses with you and let the characters experience the place so that I the reader can experience it, too. That's why I'm reading a novel instead of a screenplay.

Exposition City

Getting necessary background information into the hands of your reader is a challenge. Most writers know they don't want five densely written, information-packed paragraphs just plopped down in the middle of chapter two, so they write a nice snappy scene during which Sam and Joe discuss the exposition even though the plotline calls for them both to know all this stuff and therefore they have no really good reason to talk about it. Try very hard to let the necessary information seep into the story as needed. It's amazing how little we actually have to know in order to be hooked, and it's amazing how much more fun it is to slip exposition into the story through secrets and lies than laying it all out in one place.

Over-the-Top Emotions

To many beginning writers, louder is better. People in early scenes shout and sob, scream and cry their way through the action like scenery-chewing actors even though there isn't that much for them to yell about

The Storyboard

Stage Setup
- Time:
- Place:
- Season:
- Weather or indoor conditions:
- Sounds:
- Smells:
- Sights:
- Tastes and touches:

Characters
- Who's there?
- What's their relationship?
- Whose viewpoint is it?
- Who wants something?

Props
- What physical objects surround the characters?
- What details of their surroundings do they notice and/or comment on?
- How do the characters' clothes reflect personality?
- Does any physical object remind someone of the past?
- Does any physical object take on symbolic meaning?

---

yet. Let the emotions, like the actions, build by showing simmering resentments underlying the shouting matches that ideally belong in Arc Three. Anger alone does not a conflict make.

Lots of Talk, No Action

We need some sort of decision or resolution at the end of a scene. We may all attend meetings at work where much is discussed and nothing is ever decided, but that shouldn't happen in a work of fiction. We can't table the discussion for another meeting; we need movement *now* and the scene must end in such a way that further action is inevitable. Don't make a phone appointment to see a witness, get in the car and go there. Now.

Action

- What's the large action?
- What smaller actions make up the large action?
- How does the character's performance of the action reflect character?
- How does the other character react to action?

Dialogue

- What do the characters talk about?
- What's going on under the surface?
- How does each character's dialogue reflect personality?
- Do they disagree? Could they if they tried?

Outcome

- What's the outcome for the main scene character?
  (*Best* outcomes are "yes, but" and "no, and furthermore.")
- What does the main character feel, have, or want at the beginning of the scene?
- What has the character gained or lost?
- How does the gain/loss affect the character's overall story goal?
- What's the climax of the scene?
- Do you have a curtain line? Could you?

The Incredible Jumping Conflict
Our hero confronts his girlfriend, who also happens to be his boss as well as his main suspect in the death of their co-worker. Too many conflicts in one scene leave the reader wondering which one is really important right now. When a scene has several characters in it, try to focus on two main ones and let the others take a subordinate role for the moment. We need one scene goal and one resolution of that goal per scene, no more.

Trailing Off into Nothingness
"And then I went home and opened a can of soup for dinner and did my laundry and settled in to watch a little television." So what? If the scene ended back at the Fat Man's penthouse, then *stop*. Give the scene a beginning, middle, and snappy end that doesn't just trail off because, God forbid, the reader should miss a fascinating account of what the detective

ate for dinner. Now, if eating that lonely dinner gives the detective time to reflect upon what he's learned and what he's going to do next, then we have a reaction and that's worth something, but if all it is is soup, it goes.

Failing to Link Back to Main Plotline or Subplot

My great insight into how to end chapters came from Dick Francis's *Reflex*. It's a nice complex read with five plotlines, one major and several minor but all interconnected. What Francis did was to end every chapter on a note that harked back to one of these plotlines, leading to last lines like "I wondered what I'd do with the rest of my life when my racing days were over." We were never far from the main thrust of the story and what it all meant to our hero. Writers who leave subplots dangling without bringing them back home run the risk of losing readers who wonder what they're reading this stuff for.

Cliffhangers

Here's where the distinction between scenes and chapters comes in handy. It's okay to end a chapter in the middle of a scene. It's also okay to combine several scenes into one chapter.

This gives a writer extraordinary flexibility. You can start a scene in chapter five and break just at the point where one character pulls a gun on another, or where our detective finds a body, or where our suspense hero discovers that the man she thought was her father adopted her.

Cut to chapter six, even though our character is exactly where we left her in chapter five.

Why do this? Why not just keep writing and forget about the chapter break?

Because one of the things a writer loves most is forcing the reader to read more than she intended to. "Can I *please* just finish this chapter?" I used to beg my mother when she wanted my help in the kitchen, and you can believe that any chapter that closed with a cliffhanger earned a few sneaky peeks into the next chapter in spite of my promise. That's part of what makes suspense, that sense of absolutely having to know what happens next, and ending the chapter in mid-scene just as the exciting part comes is an important trick of the trade.

It shouldn't be overused. Cutting in mid-scene for the discovery of one body is great; when it happens the third time, the reader is likely to yawn instead of gasp. Too much artificial drama kills the real drama that ought to come from character, situation, and setting.

"Meanwhile, back at the ranch," is a device writers working in multiple viewpoint can use to add to the cliffhanger suspense. Now not only is the reader left hanging while one character is in danger, but the writer switches the scene to another part of the story, another viewpoint character, so that we have to wait even longer to find out whether or not Pauline will be run over by that train whose tracks she's tied to. And if the writer's really on top of her game, she won't leave the ranch until something else dramatic happens there, and then she'll leave that story at the most exciting point.

Narrative—The Alternative to Scene

What about those parts of the story that aren't written in scene form? How can the writer use narrative without lapsing into "telling" instead of "showing"?

Very few writers choose a totally scene-oriented style. One who does is Gregory Mcdonald, the author of the *Fletch* series. Try picking up one of his fast-paced books to get a sense of what a novel without narrative looks like, and you'll see that while it's fun to read, it's also something you wouldn't want all novels to look like. Narrative has its place.

Two questions about narrative: When should you use it and how do you put spin on the narrative ball?

Uses of Narrative

- To set the scene or establish location. Emma Lathen, who wrote wonderful Wall Street mysteries, always opened the books with deftly written "portraits" of the financial district that give the reader a context for the murder to come.

- To cover a lot of temporal ground in a short space of words. The scene takes place in real time, but the whole book can't unless it covers a three-hour stretch of time. One of my favorite "time-cruncher" narrative lines occurs in Grace Paley's short story, "Ruthie and Edie." One segment of the story takes place in the Bronx when the girls are children; the next segment begins, "Fifty years later, they sat in Faith's kitchen..." Fifty years—gone in a puff of smoke, in three words from the hidden narrator.

- To create the reaction section after a scene, during which the character reflects on the scene and chooses the next action. While it's possible to show a character's inner thoughts while the scene is going on, once the character is alone, we're not quite in scene any longer. We're summing up what he's thinking, what he's doing, and what he plans to do next, and that's narrative.

Putting Spin on the Narrative Ball

- Narrative doesn't mean just telling the reader what's happened. "And then he went home and ate his soup" is boring narrative. "He stared at the soup, which lay cold and congealed in the bowl. He'd come a long way from the days when he ate in four-star restaurants, handed twenties to parking lot attendants, squired beautiful women who wore dresses that sparkled in the candlelight. His whole life had come down to this: cold soup by the light of a black-and-white television set." He's still eating the same old soup, but now the soup *means something*. Making it mean something is what the art of narrative is all about.

- Using language is part of beefing up the narrative. Bring out the vocabulary. Never let a wimpy verb creep in, or a generic noun. Cut and trim to the point where every single observation is a "closely observed detail" (in the words of John Gardner) that furthers the reader's understanding of the overarching emotional situation.

- Emotion is the key. Whose emotion? Sometimes it's the character through whose sensibilities that particular narrative is filtered. Sometimes it's the emotion a hidden narrator brings to the tale. (The "voice" Emma Lathen used to describe Wall Street was one of an anthropologist with a wry sense of humor describing particularly outlandish tribal customs.)

I know what you're thinking—"I'm supposed to create full-bodied scenes with deep character development, realistic dialogue, and dead-on description. Then I'm supposed to write narrative connectors that sparkle with wit and contain closely observed details. At the same time, I'm moving my plot toward its plot point, I'm planting and concealing clues, I'm keeping secrets and creating suspense, and I'm hurtling toward a take-no-prisoners ending."

Sounds like work, doesn't it?

The good news is that you don't have to do it all in a single draft. You can plan the writing you're going to do and you can revise once you're finished. But no matter how you approach the craft of writing, you will at some point have to examine your sentences, word by word, to make sure they're doing the job you want done. Editing at the sentence level can make the difference between getting published and being seen as an amateur without a sophisticated, developed style.

Style

Novels, whether mystery or suspense, are made up of arcs. Arcs are made up of chapters, which are made up of scenes. Scenes in turn are comprised of paragraphs and sentences.

Sentences are composed of words; the choice of the right words in the best arrangement is what we call *style.*

Parts of Speech and How They Create Style
Verbs

Verbs are the lifeblood of fiction. People do things, and the way they do them says a great deal about who they are. So give the reader as clear a picture as possible by using verbs that really say something. Let your characters strut instead of just walking, let sounds crackle and pound, let waves and vehicles crash and thud and shudder.

Get the "hads" out of your prose. Too many beginning writers clutter their sentences with weak verbs and unnecessary past tenses. "I walked down the street" is fine; "I had walked" is seldom needed. Let your characters do what they're going to do; don't let them "begin" to do it.

Nouns

Nouns should be as specific as possible, which is why a lot of writers use brand names to say something about character, which can work in some cases but can also be a lazy way of avoiding real character creation. Narrative especially needs what the great writing teacher John Gardner calls "the closely observed detail," the one little thing that sums up a human being. Raymond Chandler was especially good at this; some of his minor characters stay in our memories a long time because he chose one perfect detail to convey their essence.

Make a list. Use the storyboard to write down everything you "see" in Mr. Big's office. Then hone the list by cutting the obvious, such as autographed pictures with the mayor and oversized ebony desks. Then pick one thing you haven't read anywhere else before and make that the centerpiece of your description.

Adjectives

If your nouns are nice and specific, why do you need adjectives? Because even a great noun can't always say it all. There's a difference between brand new sneakers and down-at-heel, unpolished oxfords. Like nouns, adjectives need specificity to be effective. "A pretty girl" doesn't say much, and neither does "intelligent green eyes." Give me a closely observed detail about that pretty face, or better yet, a mannerism that tells me the girl knows she's pretty. Give me a metaphor for the green eyes, or better yet, show me behavior that indicates intelligence.

Like medication, adjectives shouldn't be overused. Three in a row is probably too many, unless they say three very different things about the object or person being described.

Adverbs

Adverbs are a lazy way out. Part of writing one's way into the story (more on this in chapter ten) is getting it down on paper as fast as you can, so mistakes are made. People walk "quickly," and say things "sarcastically" as a form of shorthand so that the writer remembers what she wanted to say without stopping to find a better way to say it right then.

But in the rewrite, those adverbs need to be replaced by verbs that tell the whole story all by themselves and by dialogue that actually conveys sarcasm without having to tell the reader that's what it was meant to be. Let the character hustle or skitter or edge his way through the crowd, let him scramble like a quarterback or sidle like a snake. Let the dialogue speak for itself; if it's sarcastic enough, we won't need to be told that's what it was. Cut the adverbs and your prose will tighten like a Hollywood star after her first face lift.

Metaphors can be fun. More fun than adverbs, anyway.

Pronouns

A second reader helps with pronoun problems. You need someone to circle that third or fourth "he" and put a note in the margin: "who he?" Then you'll know to go back into the sentence and clarify whether Mr. Big Bad Guy shot your hero or the other way around.

Sentence Structure

I know what the problem is. We're writing prose, which means that one word comes before another word, and so on. But we want to show a scene in which a man picks up a stick and talks to his friend *at the exact same time.* So we write, "Picking up the stick, John turned to Sam," or "As he picked up the stick, John turned to Sam."

All right, that's not terrible, but it is clunky and the truth is, the reader doesn't actually care whether or not these two actions are happening at the same time. We've been reading for a long, long time now and we know that just because we read one thing first and the other thing second doesn't mean they happened separately. It's a convention, so that writing, "John picked up the stick. He turned to Sam and said" isn't going to confuse us.

This comes up a lot in action scenes. We want to create the movie action experience, so our characters slide out of car seats, grab guns out of glove compartments, shoot off a round, duck the rounds that are coming back at them, and shelter their companions all in the same overheated sentence. It doesn't make for fast-paced writing, just confused writing.

Short sentences that tell us precisely what's happening have more punch than long convoluted exercises in subordinate clauses. Any time your action prose is larded with "as" and "-ing" and "while," you're killing the jarring sense of sudden danger that is at the heart of action.

Stupid Dialogue Tricks

Dialogue should be the most natural thing in the world. I mean, we talk every day, right? We know how to do it and we hear other people doing it all the time, so how hard can it be to put talking on the page and make it sound natural?

Harder than it looks for a few reasons. One is that if we put in all the banal, silly, dumb stuff people really talk about in real life we'd bore our readers to death. A little bit of reality goes a long way on the printed page. Another problem is telling the reader who's talking so that they don't get confused. For some bizarre reason a lot of writers think they have to do much more than just identifying the speaker in order to write like real writers.

So when it comes to revising dialogue and its attendant prose, here are a few things to avoid:

- Repeating what the speaker just said. ("Harvey, don't you ever do that again," she scolded.) We just heard the character doing the scolding; why tell the reader that was what she was doing? Why not cut "scolded" and replace it with something more interesting, such as a description. ("Harvey, don't you ever do that again." Mama stood on the porch in her fluffy pink bunny slippers, her hair in rollers, hands on her hips.) We know it was Mama who spoke; we don't need "Mama said as she stood on the porch" or "said Mama, standing on the porch." Cut the extraneous little words and go for straightforward sentences.

- Working overtime to find substitutes for "said." Characters who giggle, snort, chuckle, grimace, muse, mumble, or screech their way through dialogue should be taken out and shot. Dead. Again, just tell me what the character said, and if you want to add behavior, put it in the next sentence. ("I don't know why you think I had anything to do with the murder." She giggled and fingered her pink sweater; her nails were bitten to the quick.)

- Using adverbs to make up for weak dialogue. Cut every single adverb and then look at the actual dialogue. Make it sound the way you told the reader it was.

- Stopping the dialogue flow to give us interior monologue reacting to every word the non-viewpoint character says. Let the viewpoint character say what he's thinking, or, if his thoughts are the opposite of what he's saying, let him internalize once or twice, but let the dialogue take precedence.

- Dialect is out. Hinting at a character's ethnic background or regional origins by very subtle means is in. The occasional foreign word or "y'all" will do, and by all means, don't spell funny. Editors hate funny spelling. So do intelligent readers.

Scene and style, then, are the basic ingredients of a well-written, entertaining novel. Mastering the basics of scene creation and working toward a writing style that expresses your personality are important aspects of becoming the writer you want to be.

How you go about putting words on the page depends upon the kind of writer (perhaps even the kind of person) you already are.

10. Outliners and Blank-Pagers

The Writing Process

THERE ARE two kinds of writers: those who want a detailed outline in place before they start to write actual prose, and those whose creative juices flow when they contemplate a blank piece of paper waiting to be filled with story. The second group regards an outline as a straitjacket, claiming it ruins the spontaneity they see as integral to the creative process. The first group looks upon the outline as a kind of first draft, a place where all the bugs can be ironed out before they have 170 pages under their belts. Each group tends to regard the other with suspicion: surely nobody could be crazy enough to write *that* way?

I call these different types of writers Outliners and Blank-pagers. My experience teaching writing tells me that most people are very clear which group they belong to: Outliners instinctively gravitate to the index card section of the stationery store. They are the people who never go to the grocery store without a shopping list (preferably one organized according to each aisle of said store), make reservations when they go on vacation, and carry huge day planners or tiny Palm Pilots so they can schedule dinner dates well in advance. Blank-pagers, in contrast, travel without reservations, seeking the adventure of not knowing in advance where they'll be spending the night. They like the excitement of living as well as writing in the moment.

Mystery writers tend to be Outliners, although there are notable exceptions to this non-rule. The form demands a certain precision; outlining is one way of testing the logical underpinnings of the mystery before committing oneself to paper. You can plot out the murder in a straight-line narrative, make clue packages and timelines. You can draw up maps, family trees, and dossiers for each suspect. You can begin chapter one with a file folder crammed with detailed information.

Suspense, according to Joe Gores, "should never be outlined." His view—and it's a view endorsed by Elmore Leonard and Stephen King—is that the hero's frantic search for a way out of his dilemma is best created by the writer putting himself in that same dilemma. Write your way into a tight corner, these Blank-pagers recommend, and then write your way out of it in the cleverest way you can think of.

Neither way is wrong or right. Some writers begin in blank page and then outline when they hit page 100 or so; others draft outlines as rough guides and then throw them away when they get into the Zone. The key is to discover which basic process works for you and modify it as needed.

Expansion and Contraction

Writing a novel involves cycles of expansion and contraction. At the beginning, both Outliners and Blank-pagers are likely to be in the expansive mode, casting their nets wide for inspiration. Could the murdered man have been a blackmailer? Why not? Or was he just someone who knew too much? Let's try that on for size. Or perhaps it wasn't Harry who was murdered after all; his wife, Betty, would make an even better corpse. Or, no, not Betty—how about Melanie, the mistress?

What mistress? Harry didn't have a mistress when I started this novel.

But it would be so much more interesting if he did.

And it would be even more interesting if Betty opened the door to the bedroom she shares with Harry only to find her rival's body, clad in a silk slip, lying dead on the chenille.

At this stage, the writer is open to possibility. Whether she is jotting her ideas on index cards or scribbling prose onto the page, she is letting her muse take her where it will. She is expanding.

At some point in the writing process, the wide net of expansion must give way to the focus of contraction. The Outliner organizes his material in advance of writing; he makes connections between characters before putting them on the page. This process is contractive; it leaves out anything that doesn't serve to move the story as a whole. Everything that's left is either part of the main plot, a subplot, or a red herring.

Wheat's Law of the Conservation of Plot Points

Somewhere in this process, the stolen diamond necklace that started the story may drop by the wayside. Or it may become a subplot, a clue, a red herring. According to Wheat's Law of the Conservation of Plot Points, nothing's wasted. If a mystery writer creates four solid suspects for the crime, and in the course of letting the vision change she decides to go with Number Three instead of One as the real killer, she hasn't wasted her time working up a straight-line narrative for One, because that will make a splendid red herring. How can the reader help but be convinced that One is the real killer, when the writer herself believed it for a while? The clue packages that point the reader toward One will make for a stronger red herring than the writer would have had if she'd stuck to her original plan. And Three as the killer will come as just the kind of surprise she had in mind in the first place.

Some writers follow Raymond Chandler's advice that when things go slack, introduce a man with a gun. Don't bother explaining who he is, or connecting him to anything right away—just send him through the door and let the characters react to him. Other writers suggest, "Deliver a package." What's in the package? Anything from a severed hand to a bomb—just so it's exciting and leads to more action on the page.

The conservation-of-plot-points part comes when the writer needs to connect that severed hand to the rest of the story. How *can* it connect when the writer had no idea it was going to happen until it appeared, as if by magic, on the P.I.'s battered oak desk?

Have a look at Lawrence Block's novel *The Burglar Who Traded Ted Williams*. Stolen baseball cards, valuable ones, are at the center of the story. It seems that everyone Bernie Rhodenbarr comes in contact with knows about these cards, even though there is no apparent reason they should know. What appears to be the kind of coincidence writing teachers warn you about turns out to be no coincidence when Block later reveals the connections among these seemingly unrelated characters.

Hidden connections between seemingly unrelated people and things conserve your favorite characters and clues by integrating them fully into the story. They're no longer irrelevant wanderings away from the main point; they take us right back to that point, even if they get there by a circular path. That wonderfully quirky old antique dealer you can't bear to leave on the cutting-room floor can stay in the story if he turns out to be the grandfather of the client's girlfriend. It won't be a coincidence if the girlfriend suggested him as the expert the P.I. ought to see about those stolen Ming vases.

The Outliner's Process

There's an upside and a downside to both processes. If you're an Outliner, you can spend a huge amount of time making ready to write without actually writing. Some outliners make themselves crazy with pre-planning. Every character has a history, every location is detailed with precision, whether it matters to the story or not. Research eats up an enormous amount of time for some Outliners, who may compound their mistake by trying to cram as much of it into their books as possible.

If preparation enhances the final product, it's time well spent; if it doesn't, it's vamping.

Vamping till ready: the piano player knocks out a jaunty little tune while he's waiting for the performer to step onto the stage. If the performer's a little late, the piano player repeats the vamp. He keeps on repeating it until it's time to go into the actual number. If he vamps for too long a time, the audience begins to clamor for the performer. The same is true of outlining—at some point you must begin the actual prose. You must write CHAPTER ONE on a piece of paper and spill some lifeblood on the page just like every other writer on the planet.

The Outliner needs to be aware that the tendency to want everything to be perfect before CHAPTER ONE hits the page is a fantasy. No matter how hard he works to get everything in place, chapter one is a draft. It will change. There is no such thing as perfect. There comes a time when the Outliner has to let go of the preparation mode and get into writing mode. He's got to stop vamping and start writing.

The Changing Vision

The first step is to realize that while a writer begins a book with a vision, that vision is bound to change as the book takes shape. The Outliner thinks she sees the book as a whole, sitting like a pot of gold at the end of the writing rainbow. The operative words here are "she thinks." In truth, the Outliner can't see the finished book as clearly as she believes she does; there will be changes she can't imagine at the beginning, and if she's writing a living novel instead of a classroom exercise, she'd better let them happen.

Novels are big. They take a long time to write. And in the course of that writing, things change. Pieces of the Outliner's vision stubbornly refuse to fall into place; what seemed inevitable now seems contrived and must be rethought. You look back at chapter one from the vantage point of chapter seven and long to rip it up and start over.

What's going on?

The vision changes. The vision grows and alters as the writer works herself deeper into the story. The best writers let this happen. They open themselves to a new vision; they permit the book to grow and shape itself according to an altered perception.

The Outliner's Toolbox

The process of pre-planning can occur in a number of ways. Rick Boyer, who won an Edgar award for *Billingsgate Shoal*, gets one of those marbled hardcover essay notebooks and fills it with a scenario of the story. His scenario may include maps and drawings, and sums up the entire action. He handwrites it, although he uses a word processor when it comes to the actual prose. It's one way of gaining overview, of managing the tremendous amount of information a writer needs to carry in his head in order to write an entire novel.

Margaret Maron, on the other hand, fills folders with material for each chapter; when it comes time to write, say, chapter three, she'll have notes and pictures cut from magazines and articles about the topic and anecdotes she heard from a local wise woman. That folder is a kind of outline, even though it is used to stimulate the filling of a blank page.

Maron has also created a detailed family tree for her main character, Judge Deborah Knott (who has ten brothers, so it's quite a tree), as well as a map of her fictional Colleton County, North Carolina. Particularly if you're developing a series, having visual aids to help you keep things consistent will pay off in the long run.

Some really experienced writers—Lawrence Block and Robert B. Parker come to mind—do it all in their heads. Block "blocks out" his story (okay, take me out and shoot me) and when he has it fairly well set in his mind, he checks into a motel, plugs in his laptop, and bangs the script out in a week or two. The speed of his writing is made possible by the months of thinking work he did before the check-in.

While it's hard to call that outlining, it is a way of pre-planning what's going to be written down. It is not the free-floating style of the true

Blank-pager; the in-the-head writer is culling and editing as he goes, tossing out what doesn't work before it has the chance to clutter up the disk or the page.

The essence of outlining is throwing away. The Blank-pager spills all her ideas onto a page and culls later; the Outliner narrows the focus, consolidates characters, drops subplots before committing himself to prose.

What do you do with the stuff that's left over? Some writers make a file of out-takes, material that isn't useful for this book but might be recycled into the next novel or into a short story. The truth is that most of the stuff that hits the cutting-room floor never gets recycled, but that's not what's important; what's important is that it doesn't go into *this* book. A writer in the contractive stage has to be willing to let go of anything that isn't moving the central storyline.

One of the benefits of outlining is that the culling process happens before the writer has committed himself to actual prose. It's a lot easier to lay aside a few index cards than to excise whole scenes involving a character you no longer want in the story.

Opening Up the Story

Sometimes a writer must move from a contraction phase back into expansion. This can happen to an Outliner whose preplanned scenes don't work on the page the way he hoped they would while in outline form.

I had a clue once, a really brilliant and wonderful clue given to me by my local Brooklyn pizza parlor. They made specialty pizzas, and one of my favorites was rosemary chicken. Long spikes of rosemary on top of white-meat chicken spread out on a crisp pizza crust—tasty and unusual. So I decided the victim in my book would have eaten that pizza before she died; it would be in her stomach, and would point to the fact that she'd eaten at a certain pizza parlor that served this unusual dish. I used to go and eat "clue pizza" and enjoy it even more knowing how I was going to use it in my book.

The trouble was that when I went to write the scene, I realized that the victim had no reason to go to this particular pizza parlor, which was nowhere near the scene of her death, except to eat this pizza and give my detective a clue. What had looked so terrific in outline had become contrived and illogical in the context of the story.

If you read the finished book (*Fresh Kills*), you will find no reference to rosemary chicken pizza. I still mourn my pizza clue, but the good of the book as a whole demanded that I deviate from the outline and open up to a new way of finding Amber's killer.

I had to move from the contraction phase of writing according to the outline, and go back into expansion in order to find new clues to replace my lost pizza clue. I had to brainstorm, to cast my net wide, to open myself up to a new set of what-ifs in order to solve a problem I thought I had already solved.

Outliners can also move back into expansion by means of freewriting. This is writing without a plan, writing off the record. I've done it for different reasons at different stages of the writing process. Once I freewrote a scene between a father and daughter on the daughter's tenth birthday. This scene wasn't in the book because the daughter was fourteen when the action of the novel took place, but by letting myself see a glimpse of the father-daughter relationship at an earlier stage, I added depth to the portraits that did end up between the covers of the book. I've also written my way into certain characters by freewriting about them in their own voices, even though they will only be seen in the finished book through the eyes of my first-person main character. Both methods involve a foray into expansion during the contractive phase of writing-to-outline.

Do the Opposite

Does this sound like I'm telling you to do the opposite of what you've been doing?

If so, you're getting the point. When you find yourself blocked, what you've been doing is taking you down a path that leads to frustration, so trying the opposite ought to end the frustration. The trouble is, it also makes you nervous because it's alien to your instinctive nature as a writer.

The Outliner hates giving up that tightly knit structure, yet opening up and adding a new character, a new subplot, another clue package, is just what the book needs. Micromanaging your characters even more than you already have leads to dry, dull characters without a spontaneous thought in their heads.

Trust is the key here. Trust in yourself and trust in your overriding vision. Trust that you won't be losing golden words and startling plot developments; you'll be gaining richer characters and even better twists and turns. Trust that there's more where the old stuff came from, that you have the talent and depth to take your material to the max and you don't have to settle for something your heart tells you isn't working.

The Blank-Pager's Toolbox _____

Suspense writers are more likely than mystery people to be Blank-pagers. The suspense writer likes writing her character into a corner and then extricating her by sheer wit. For a wonderful example of how this process works, try reading Stephen King's *Misery*, in which a writer is forced to create his story by the blank-page method. Blank-pagers are wonderful at starting books, at creating gripping situations that bring the reader into the story.

The crunch comes when the story has to go somewhere. Blank-pagers often come into my classes complaining that they've written one hundred pages of a novel and stopped because they had no central plotline. Great scenes, but no payoff. Several threads of story that never wove themselves into a coherent whole. The downside of spontaneity is that a novel needs a spine, and the Blank-pager may not understand how to give it one.

How can Blank-pagers pull their stories together without losing the spark of spontaneity?

Blank-pagers go through a contraction process, too. Some don't do it until they've finished an entire first draft. They want to work their way through the story step by step, then set the manuscript aside for a bit and go back in with a hacksaw. They can't decide what to leave out and what to emphasize in chapter one until they've seen how the final chapter plays out.

But some Blank-pagers don't want to wait until the end. They are the ones who come into class with ten chapters of a book that, when looked at correctly, will emerge as three or four stories piled on top of one another. There's the storyline about the stolen diamond necklace; there's the mysterious package delivered to the house; there's Harry and his mistress meeting for the last time at a seedy bar near the bus station; there's a man at the bus station asking for directions and saying something about "paying back Melanie." How does it all hang together? And who is that man at the bus station?

The first thing the Blank-pager in this situation must do is stop writing. The natural tendency of the Blank-pager is to solve all writing problems by scaring up a new storyline; all this does is add another wing to an already sprawling house. (If you've ever been to the Winchester Mystery House in San Jose, you'll see the architectural equivalent of this process. Sarah Winchester, widow of the inventor of the Winchester rifle, was told she'd die when she finished building her house, so—she never finished! She built stairways to nowhere, rooms too tiny to stand up in, and innumerable windows peering into blank walls. Not a house you'd want to live in—and not a book you'd want to read.)

The second thing the writer must do is reread what she already has and ask herself which of her storylines excites her the most. Is it the diamond necklace? Is it the relationship between Melanie, the mistress, and her mother? Is it that scene where Betty broke down in tears as she confessed that she'd known about Harry's mistress for years but never said anything?

One of the storylines is going to be more interesting to you than the others. Maybe it's the last one to enter the mix; maybe it's the one that's gotten the most ink. Whatever the reason for choosing one, the important thing is to decide which storyline will dominate the book.

Now comes the hard part. Out come the scissors and paste. Everything that doesn't relate to the newly chosen main story *goes.* You may open an out-takes file and put all the nonusable prose into it in hopes that it will form the germ of a second book or a short story, but the important thing now is to get it out of the novel. Only the scenes that move the main story will remain—and the ten chapters you started with may boil down to three and a half.

Don't worry. Your three and a half chapters will form the nucleus of a book you have a chance of actually finishing.

Give Your Characters Jobs

After a writer in the contractive stage has identified a main story and culled out any storylines that don't move that main story, she can begin to focus on character. Are all the characters employed? Do they have jobs to do, and are they doing them?

By "jobs" I don't mean what they do when they leave their fictional houses; I mean what is their role in the story? How do they move the plot, develop character, act as ally or opponent to the main character? If the book is a mystery, the major characters will be suspects, and as such, they must act suspicious. They must lie, they must refuse to answer questions, they must possess motive and means and opportunity. A party scene filled with fascinating characters speaking witty dialogue is not an asset to the mystery unless that dialogue is being spoken by suspects acting suspicious. As mere window dressing, it goes.

In the same vein, incidents, objects, and settings should be examined to see whether they could produce clues for the detective. The Outliner will already have her clue packages ready to slip into the scenes; the Blank-pager may wish to reread her prose and highlight anything that might become a clue with a little reshaping. The Blank-pager might want to use a few Outliner tools like maps and timelines to help focus what he's already written.

Connections between characters can also help focus the story; the Outliner undoubtedly knows that Ted is really Sarah's former lover, but this may come as a shock to the Blank-pager, who has just discovered this fact through writing a scene in which Ted suddenly confessed this hitherto unknown connection. The Blank-pager will want to reread former chapters involving both Ted and Sarah and make notes for revision to enhance the relationship, which will tighten the story considerably.

Suspense characters have jobs, too. In the early stages of the story, characters may be shown to be supportive of the hero—which will make their later betrayal and abandonment of her all the more poignant. The Blank-pager may reread her material and highlight characters to be developed into allies or obstacles in revision.

Writers are gardeners of words. We plant, weed, fertilize, trim, and hoe only to receive as the highest compliment the praise that "it looks so natural." Making your writing read as if it flowed effortlessly from your keyboard takes hard work.

Weeding

Blank-pagers write their way into the story. When introducing a new character, they're likely to write five pages of backstory because they're learning it as they write. This leaves them with a lot of unusable prose, which is no sin in a first draft, but that unusable prose has no business surviving to a second draft. It has to go. Pulling it out and leaving the good stuff is one basic task all Blank-pagers have to learn.

Scissors and paste are necessary tools of the writer's trade even in the cyber-age, mainly because you simply can't see enough on the screen. You need to do big-picture revision by making piles on the floor or table—one for each arc, to begin with. All that backstory, all those flashbacks you loaded into your first draft Arc One need to be moved to the second and third piles, to become integrated into your second draft Arcs Two and Three.

Once you've done this at the arc level, it's time to revise each and every scene.

Pull out everything that doesn't work. Strip your manuscript of all extraneous material, be it subplot or information or description. If it isn't moving the story in some way, it goes. Whole paragraphs, pages, chapters may litter the floor; that doesn't matter so long as your plants have room to grow.

Once you've done that preliminary work, it's time to look at what's left.

Nurturing the Seedlings

Even some of the good stuff may have to go. Two characters who play essentially the same role in the hero's life = one too many.

Any character without a job needs to either get one or leave the story. Play them or trade them—but don't let them take up space without contributing to the overall story.

Sharpen the scenes by cutting as much filler as you can. We don't usually need to follow the detective as he gets from here to there; just take us to where the scene begins and start there. Cut those little "and then I went home" tails off the scenes and give them zippier closing lines. Cut long descriptions of people or places and telescope the action into as concise and punchy a format as possible. Watch out for walk-on characters that dissipate the tension between the important characters.

Check the subplots for relevance to the through line. If a subplot seems unconnected with the main story, then you have two choices: connect it or lose it. Since you didn't lose it in the weeding process, you've decided to connect it. Now's the time—how can that greedy brother-in-law who stole from the family business possibly relate to the larger tale?

Maybe the entire story is about greed and what it does to people, so the brother-in-law subplot acts as a low-rent counterpoint to the world-class greed of the big villain. And the brother-in-law's gambling problem, which led him to embezzle, makes him the perfect pawn for Mr. Big Bad Guy, so *he's* the one who sent our hero that dead fish and warned him to stay away from Mr. Big.

One subplot saved.

I know—you're getting worried that all this cutting will leave you with a 125-page book, and you know that's not enough.

Relax. Thinning the seedlings is only the first part of the exercise.

Fertilizing

Now that you have less prose to work with, it's time to strengthen that prose as much as possible. Go back to the storyboard and re-ask some of the same questions:

- Have I used enough sensory language in my description?

- Does my description of place adequately reflect the inherent dangers that are going to become overwhelmingly important in Arc Four?

- Does my description include my viewpoint character's emotional response to this place?

- Have I left out any logistical setup information the reader has to know in order to make the hero's victory over evil in this place believable?

- Have I used absolutely every interesting aspect of this place somewhere in the story?

- What things are in this place that can or will be used later on? (We *don't* suddenly discover that there's a nice cache of weapons hidden in the old cave in chapter twenty; we'd better know it's there a lot earlier than that if we don't want our reader throwing the book against the wall.)

- Are there any associations, or memories associated with the place, that could give rise to some nice secrets or emotional resonance later on?

Do the same with character. If my villain is going to turn out to be a greedy man killing and betraying people for money, let's see some of that hunger for material goods early on. It may be a subtle reference to always flying first class or a silk shirt or a flashy car, but it needs to be planted early for us to get the full flavor.

Revision

Revision: some writers hate it, others embrace it like a lover. Either way, it's a flat-out necessity if a writer wants to move from the amateur "I love to write but when it gets too hard I just start another project" stage to the "I'm going to make this book as good as I possibly can no matter how much work it takes" determination that separates the pros from the wannabes.

How much revision does the average writer do? How many drafts does it take to go from rotten first draft (and it's important to realize that *all* first drafts are rotten) to award-winning, critically acclaimed best-seller?

It depends. The only thing one can say for certain is that producing a publishable novel is a long-haul proposition and that you have to revise until the book is as close as you can bring it to absolutely, totally perfect.

I agree with Jack Nicholson, whose motto is "Everything counts." That's what he said when he was awarded the American Film Institute's Lifetime Achievement Award, and it applies to writing as well as to acting. Everything, from characters to commas, from whether or not New York's Fifth Avenue is one-way going south or north to the exact properties of atropine, counts.

Why?

Because one little mistake can kick the reader out of the story. Suddenly she's not lost in a dream, she's reading a book and the characters aren't real anymore, they're just funny little black marks on a white page and you've lost her.

The Good-Enough Chapter One

Premature revision is a major cause of difficulties among beginning writers. They work chapter one to the point of exhaustion, trying to make it as perfect as possible, and then they wonder why their stamina fails by the time they reach chapter four.

The leading cause of premature revision among writers is writing teachers.

I know because I am one. My students submit a perfectly dreadful draft they call chapter one. I read it and make extensive comments on it. They rewrite it and resubmit it. I make more comments. They rewrite it again, I make more comments, and—

Well, you see the problem. The student wants a nice big gold star on her paper and I want to earn my princely salary as a teacher, so we play this little game, both of us pretending that if I give enough feedback the student can achieve perfect chapter one-ness.

She can't.

And I can't help her do it, because neither of us, at this stage of the process, has the slightest idea what the perfect chapter one for this book looks like. All she can do is write the good-enough chapter one, and all I can do for her is recognize that good-enough chapter one when I see it.

The good-enough chapter one allows the writer to keep moving, which is all she needs at this point in time. It sets up enough of the story to be going on with, it introduces the characters in such a way that we care enough to keep reading. It may well be that when the writer reaches Plot Point One, she can look back and realize that the story didn't really start until chapter three. She can then lop off her early chapters and recognize the former chapter three as the new, improved chapter one, but there was no way on God's earth she could have done that before she actually wrote chapter three.

The Non-Revision Revision

I once had a book whose first chapter I revised to the point where my computer files contained C1a, C1b, C1c, all the way to, I swear to God, C1m. That's over half the alphabet, meaning I had thirteen, count them, 13, different versions of that chapter one bouncing around on my floppy disks.

I don't recommend this method of revision.

I also don't recommend the method used by a friend, who felt that every single change in the plot or characters mandated a thorough rewrite of every chapter that went before, so that a change in chapter eighteen had her rewriting chapter one on up.

My solution: the non-revision revision, or Notes for Revision.

You've just finished chapter three and it's wonderful, the best thing you've ever written, how could you be more clever, only the problem is that the new chapter three doesn't fit with your old chapter one. Your fingers itch with the deep desire to go in and rewrite chapter one.

Try not to. Instead, take a blank piece of paper and write at the top: Notes for Revision, C1. Then jot down all the things you'd do to chapter one if you were revising, which you're not, you're just making notes. Try to keep doing this with your early chapters until you reach Plot Point One, otherwise known as the end of Arc One.

Once you've reached the end of your first arc, you're in a much better position to revise, because you can assess all that you've put on the page in terms of that arc goal. You can see which sections move the characters toward the climax and which are just filler. You can sharpen the conflicts and define the characters in terms of their relationship to that arc goal.

Sometimes you just can't wait to revise. If your chapter one wasn't really good enough, you have to revise until it is. If you need a new scene that isn't on the page, write it and insert it between the existing scenes, but resist the urge to revise the already written material.

Writing Is Rewriting

Whether you're an Outliner or a Blank-pager, whether you prefer the expansive or the contractive phase of the process, whether you revise as you go or dash off a complete draft before you return to the scene of the crime, you must revise. Revision is the heart of the process; it's what separates the pros from those who "always wanted to write if only they had the time." Only after you're sure you've written the best book you possibly can will you be able to write the magic words THE END.

The Writing Process: Tools to Help You Finish

Two Competing Forces: Expansion and Contraction
Expansion
- "what if?"
- casting the net wide
- brainstorming
- letting characters have their way with the story

Contraction
- picking and choosing
- making connections
- giving each character a fiction "job"
- letting go of material that doesn't fit overall story

Two Kinds of Writers: Outliners and Blank-pagers
Outliners
- prepare for writing
- make connections before starting
- focus material before starting to write
- cut extraneous plots and characters before starting
- create materials that won't be in finished book (maps, dossiers, calendars)

Blank-pagers
- fall in love with an empty white page
- go where it takes them
- let characters do what they want
- use the edge that uncertainty brings
- write characters into corners and then write them out again
- save the contractive stage for revision and revise extensively

What they each have to learn:
- Outliners have to learn that there's no substitute for actual writing, that they can't control the process to the point of writing a perfect first draft, and that they have to allow for spontaneity during the writing.
- Blank-pagers have to learn to love revision, because they have so much of it to do. They also have to learn to let go of plotlines and characters that don't advance the book as a whole.

The expansive stage is easy and fun;
  it's the contractive stage that's work. So...
- focus on what turns you on *right now,* no matter what you loved before
- cut as much backstory as possible and see what's left
- consider putting two characters together to make one stronger character
- drop any character who doesn't have a "job" to do in the story
- drop all subplots that don't relate in some way to main story, or, *make* those characters and subplots related somehow
- focus on conflict and opposition to strengthen the plot; raise the stakes
- work the arcs
- think in scenes

Middlebook and how to survive it:
- increase tension by setting the stopwatch or planting the bomb—or both
- let the pendulum swing between safety and danger, trust and mistrust, in ever-increasing arcs
- build to the climax by raising stakes and closing off options until main character is *forced* to final confrontation
- "turn all the rats loose"—but tie up all subplots before Arc Four
- use mini-arcs and subplot arcs to heighten tension within big plot
- make sure every scene serves more than one purpose
- build to strong climax *and then give that climax its full value*

Revision—love it or leave the business.
- "anything that doesn't kill this book makes it stronger"
- "the-good-of-the-book-as-a-whole"—allows you to kiss that scene good-bye
- cut away scaffolding and leave the building
- work the arcs, making sure each plot point is built up to and gets full play
- the important question: what am I revising *for?*
- plan on three or four full revisions, some carpentry, some textual

Writer's Block Is a Gift—Use It Wisely

- yeah, some gift. Where can I go to return it?
- the problem with chapter four may lie in chapter eight and vice versa
- do the opposite of what you've been doing:
  if you've been expanding, try contracting
  if you've been contracting, try expanding
- go deeper into character; maybe there's a good reason your character refuses to do what you want her to do
- try freewriting on a scene that won't be in the finished book
- go over all notes, all the way back to square one, and highlight what you *love*
- let go of everything that isn't working (use the out-takes file if it helps)
- trust that you have more within you to replace what isn't working
- once in a while, go to the beach and forget about your book. Let the plot simmer on the back burner of your mind

Epilogue: Next Step, Published!

Endings Are Hard, III

"WHEN DO you write? How many hours a day do you write? Are you a morning writer? Do you have a schedule? Do you write a certain number of pages a day? Do you write on a computer or do you use a quill pen?"

Do aspiring writers ask published writers questions like these because they think there's some magic answer that spells the difference between published and not-yet published?

The Writing Zone

Perhaps they do, because the only certainty in the world of creative writing is that nobody quite knows what makes one person's words sing while someone else trying to tell the same story clunks along and struggles for expression. There are intangibles at work. There is a Zone you get into, a high not unlike the one runners are said to experience, a place where the words write you and your fingers zip along while your mind gets out of the way and lets it happen.

Getting to that state and staying there for as long as possible is the key to writing success.

Giving Yourself What You Need

What it takes for you to get there and stay there is something I can't know. I know some of the things that work for me, and I know some of the things that break the mood so much that I lose the Zone. Every writer has to find out for himself what his optimal writing conditions are and then try to create those conditions as often as possible. Ask yourself one question: What am I willing to give up for my writing?

Am I willing to sleep one hour less? Am I willing to forgo two evenings of television in favor of two evenings at the computer keyboard? Can I stop reading my favorite authors while I develop my own style? (I've found that there are certain stages of the writing process during which I simply can't pick up someone else's book, and for a woman who once read five mysteries a week, that's a hard trade-off.)

A word to the self-indulgent (and aren't we all?): Giving yourself what you need isn't the same as giving yourself what you'd like to have. Sometimes you're not in the Zone and there's no way you're going to get there, but you have to write anyway because you've got a deadline. What I do in these situations is "lay track." I know I'm not writing at my best, but I'm putting words on the page and sketching out scenes I'll go back and beef up later on. Once in a while, the Zone creeps up on me and I find myself doing more than just laying track, but even if all I've done is put down the rails, at least I've contributed to the final product.

Letting Go

The second part of giving yourself what you need is adding to your bank of experience. Writers who spend a lot of time alone in front of computers miss out on life, and life, after all, is what we're writing about.

Although I tend to agree with whoever it was who said, "Some say life is the thing, but I prefer reading," I'll admit that it feels good to get up out of the chair and enter the world after a long session with imaginary people. It feels good to use my body, to engage nature even if all that means is pulling weeds out of the front yard. It's nice to see friends, to catch up with the latest movies, to let your mind take a vacation from the intense creative process.

Preparing for Publication

Okay, I understand. That walk in the park was nice, but your brain overflows with The Book, The Whole Book, and Nothing But the Book. If you can't write the thing right this minute, at least you can plan for the next step in your writing career.

How Publishing Has Changed

Your professional career path begins with the choice of a publishing house. In today's highly concentrated corporate environment, a few mega-houses in New York City use imprints that make it appear as if there are twenty to thirty big publishers, when the truth is that there are now fewer than ten. For example, The Bertelsmann Book Group owns Random House, Ballantine, Fawcett, Bantam Doubleday Dell, Crown Books, and Knopf.

So what? Why do you care?

Once upon a time, in the good old days, your agent submitted your book to, say, Random House. Once the Random House editor turned her down, she submitted to Bantam. If they weren't thrilled, she moved on to Ballantine. She might even choose to send your manuscript as a multiple submission, querying all those editors at once and hoping that all three wanted it enough to start a nice little bidding war for the privilege of paying you an advance.

No more. Now you and your agent had better select the best imprint within the giant corporate family and pitch hard, because no bidding wars will break out between editors whose separate imprints belong to the same big house. You have a scant few opportunities to break in to mass market publication, and you'd better make the most of them.

Hence the ABC list.

The ABC List

Think of it as being asked to the prom. Who's your first choice of escort? If that boy doesn't ask you, who's next on the list? As you move down the ladder of social desirability, whom would you settle for? Is there anyone you'd rather stay home than go to the prom with?

If you're seventeen, it's good to know all this before that nerdy kid with asthma walks up and asks you to the dance and you're so flustered you say yes and then you hear that cool guy from the band really wanted to ask you but you already said yes to the dork because you felt sorry for him and here you are stuck with your D choice when you could have had at least a B.

In other words, have a game plan. Know which are the A publishers for your kind of book and which are the Ds. Then start the submission process with the As and only after all the As have turned you down move on to the Bs, and so forth. Don't let yourself be scooped up by a C publisher when A-level publication was available to you. And you can only know you could have had an A house by submitting to all the A houses and letting their editors see your work.

How can you tell an A from a D?

Research. Name recognition. Number of books on the best-seller's list. Authors you've heard of on their roster. Making sure they publish mysteries, if that's what you're writing. Any number of houses have ostensibly dropped their mystery lines, although they remain open to suspense reads that sell into the millions.

How do you know which authors they publish?

Aha—here's the part you can work on while you're recharging your writing batteries.

Go to a bookstore and look at the books on the mystery shelf. Check the suspense novels; see which houses publish books like yours. Run the authors' names through a search engine and check out the publisher's website.

Start compiling your A list based on big books with a fair amount of promotion behind them.

What's promotion? How can you tell when a publisher is pushing a certain writer?

Do you see print ads for the book in major markets? Is the book in a special place in the bookstore, not just on the shelf under the author's last name? Those cardboard book holders at the checkout counter are called "dumps" and they cost money. A publisher who buys a dump for its mystery/suspense writers is a publisher to be cherished.

Watch for "starter houses," which in publishing means houses that writers leave as soon as they sell a few books and see bigger money somewhere else. Get to know which writers started where and which houses they're at now. Starter houses are fine on your B and C lists, but they don't belong with the As.

Hard vs. Soft, Big vs. Small, Paper vs. Electronic
It used to be that if you didn't have a hardcover, you didn't have a book. Paperback original was less-than. It didn't get reviewed (still doesn't, for the most part), and it didn't get respect.

But then a strange thing happened. Writers who started soft sold an amazing number of books (*vide* John D. MacDonald) and the houses that published them decided to put them in hardcover and keep the paperback rights. The hard-soft deal was born. And the start-soft-and-work-your-way-up-to-hard career path became a well-worn trail.

So one question you'll have to answer for yourself: Do I put any paperback original houses on my A list?

The answer may depend upon what you're writing. Lightweight category mysteries (such as cozies that depend upon a gimmick) may do very well in paper and then work their way to hard by the old-fashioned method of upping the sales figures with each successive book. What this means for you the author is intensive self-promotion for the first few titles (and winning awards wouldn't hurt). Your goal is to increase sales of the paperbacks every time you come out with a new title and then lobby hard for your publisher to bring you out in hardcover.

The alternative is to go for hardcover first (or better: a hard-soft deal that guarantees you a paperback appearance.) Hardcovers are bought mainly by libraries and collectors, at least when you're not well known, but the up side is that they get reviews, and good reviews can help you reach your audience.

Your final A list will probably be the big, prestigious houses based in New York. Your B list may be a mix of hard and soft; your C will probably be the independent small presses whose books are trade paperbacks and whose advances are minuscule. This is not to say that you won't enjoy seeing your work in print or that your book won't be appreciated by a loyal audience, reviewed by the mystery publications, and eligible for awards. It is to say you won't get rich unless a major house likes what it sees and makes you an offer.

D list: the e-publishers, and the self-publishing print-on-demand options. Which is not to say that people who self-publish or who use nontraditional means aren't really published, just that these are avenues to explore after you've exhausted the more traditional means.

There is a body of opinion that "it isn't worth it anymore for a new author to go through the process of trying to get published by big traditional houses." So says romantic suspense writer Penny Sansevieri, who published her first book, *The Cliffhanger*, through Xlibris, which offers a print-on-demand option. Writers pay from $500 to $1700 to get their books in print, far less than the old-fashioned vanity presses, and Amazon.com will list an e-book for a small fee, so that the book essentially becomes available worldwide. Print-on-demand books have made it to regional best-seller's lists, and as Sansevieri also says, "the beauty of print on demand is that I can build a track record, then go to the bigger houses and say, 'Look what I can do on my own.'"

Finding Editor Right

Assuming that you prefer to explore traditional options first, you're getting a good handle on which publishers you'd like to work with. But you also realize that a letter sent To Whom It May Concern won't cut it. You need a specific editor whose taste you can predict, someone whose track record says, "I like the kind of books you write."

More research. But look on the bright side: this is what you do when you hit the inevitable I Hate This Book stage. Go to your local big-box bookstore, grab a double mocha, and glide among the shelves taking notes. Which publishers publish the writers who are most like you? Which ones have a hole in their lineup because they just lost their dog/horse/quilt/cooking/Roman/cat/gardening/Victorian mystery writer?

Now pick a book from the shelves and open it up. Check the Acknowledgments section, then peruse the dedication. What you're looking for is the "To Susie Creamcheese, Editor Extraordinaire" kind of thing, because what it tells you is that Ms. Creamcheese is a big fan of psychic mysteries and that's what you write, so why not send her the manuscript of *Seances Are Murder*?

Unless the book is in the New Books section of the store, you'd better check to see if Susie is still with MegaPublishing Group or if she's gone over to Colossal Books. You can find this information in the Writer's Digest *Writer's Market* yearbooks or in *Literary Marketplace*. Both are available in libraries, so save your money and plan to spend several afternoons looking up names you've collected from the bookstore.

Wait a minute—doesn't my agent do all this? Why am I haunting the mystery section of my bookstore in Iowa City when the New York agent who's going to represent me knows every editor within a twenty-block radius of her Madison Avenue office?

Because a writer who hands her entire career over to an agent and takes no active part in choosing her editor is a writer who isn't thinking clearly. By the time you're ready for an agent, you should be able to discuss your future publishing options with confidence. Talk to writers at conferences, meet as many agents and editors as you can, learn about the business you're about to enter, and never forget that once you've finished putting words on the page it is a business. Mind your own business.

Back to the Zone

Then get back to work. Start a Great Agent Hunt file, an ABC List file, keep adding more data as you acquire more information, but put the pre-publishing research on the back burner and get back into your writing routine.

E.M. Forster says a writer either allocates a certain number of hours per day to the job or chooses a number of pages to complete by the end of a writing session. I find that the "hours per day" option works when I'm in the outlining phase, but once I start the actual writing, setting a page number works better for me.

I'm also a spurt writer, so there are times I just glue myself to the chair and write till my fingers are ready to fall off. The dangers there are two-fold: thinking you're going to write like that every day and feeling let down when you can't, or deciding you've done so much work you might as well take a week off. If I succumb to that temptation, I'll soon find that my spurt actually cost me precious time because I've used more than the equivalent in recovering from it.

Revision time has special rhythms. It takes large chunks of time, not to mention space, to get the big-picture revision out of the way. It can't be done solely on the computer screen, and it can't be done in twenty-minute increments.

When Is It Finished? _____

You've ripped it to shreds at least three times. You've laid it out in piles on the floor and shifted papers frantically from one pile to another. You've cut and pasted, made notes for revision in at least four different colors of ink, you've shown it to all your friends and incorporated their better suggestions into your rewrite. You've worked the arcs and tinkered with your chaptering and firmed up that sagging middle. You've beefed up the ending and slashed the beginning. You've given all your characters jobs and you've linked your subplots so that nothing's hanging out there all by itself.

You've line-edited to the point where you could recite all of chapter one in your sleep. You've cut the adverbs, strengthened the verbs, and specified the nouns. You've consciously created metaphors and crafted dialogue that jumps off the page. There isn't an ounce of flab in your taut, spare prose and your title is a work of art in itself.

You've checked for errors, using your computer's spell-checker and then eyeballing the book for grammar and punctuation mistakes. You've given the book to someone else for proofreading and corrected all mistakes in the computer before printing out.

Before you, on a table or in your lap sits a pristine, clean, fresh copy that, as far as your human ability can make it, is absolutely, totally perfect.

You start to read.

You tell yourself you're reading it over one more time just to make sure there's nothing more to fix, but that isn't true.

You're reading it over one more time *because it's so damn good.*

That, my friends, is "finished."

Enjoy "finished" for a little bit. Let the pride wash over you and bask in the glow of your achievement. There is a great gulf fixed, not between the published and the not-yet-published, but between the finished and the not-yet-finished. Once you've completed an entire manuscript—and by "completed" I mean fully revised and ready to send out into the world to be seen by people not related to you—you've taken a giant step toward your goal of becoming a real writer. You can never go back to your earlier innocence. You can never whine and say, "Oh, I could never write a whole novel all by myself. It would be too hard."

You've done it. And it *was* hard. But now you know exactly how hard it is and *you know that it wasn't too hard for you to actually accomplish.* You know that any time you're truly ready to make the commitment of time, energy, and perfectionism, you can do it again.

So enjoy it.

Then start the next one.

Buckle up your seat belt and start the climb up the roller coaster, anticipating the plunge that will have you screaming in ecstatic terror (or terrified ecstasy, your choice). Enter the big clown head and turn left at the skeleton, making your way toward the Hall of Mirrors. Come back to the playground and never forget the most important thing of all when it comes to writing.

Have fun.

Selected Bibliography

This is a far from comprehensive listing of the many titles available on the subject of mystery writing. Instead, it is a quirky, personal discussion of books that taught me things about writing I needed to know and books I consider worthy assets to any writer's bookshelf. I'm a believer in self-help and in learning through reading, and I advise my students to start compiling a shelf of books they can always turn to when the going gets rough, and if there's any one thing writers can always count on, it's that the going will get rough.

I. Writer's Bookshelf Staples

Telling Lies for Fun and Profit
Lawrence Block (Arbor House, Revised Edition 1994)
   This collection of columns from *Writer's Digest* covers a range of problems common to all fiction writers, not just those of us engaged in criminal conduct. Block gives great hands-on advice with wit and humor. A book to pick up when you've hit a snag in hopes that once upon a time, Block hit the same snag and figured out how to cope with it.

Self-Editing for Fiction Writers
Renni Browne and Dave King (HarperCollins, 1993)
   If you bought only one book from this list, here's the one. Read it and apply its wisdom at any stage of the writing process, and your prose will

perk up. I can't promise that following Browne and King's suggestions will propel your manuscript out of the slush pile and into print, but ignoring their advice will have editors leaving your work on the shelf in favor of manuscripts with more polished prose.

Writing Mysteries: A Handbook by the Mystery Writers of America, 2nd ed.
Sue Grafton, editor (Writer's Digest Books 2001)

Insights from the pros abound in this collection of essays by MWA members, each writing about an aspect of the craft at which they excel. Here's Michael Connelly on creating characters, Tony Hillerman on the joys of being a Blank-pager, Carolyn Wheat on developing style.

The Art of Fiction: Notes on Craft for Young Writers
John Gardner (Knopf 1984)

This revered classic is geared toward literary rather than popular fiction, but Gardner's advice applies to mystery and suspense writing, too. His gems linger in the mind; he's the teacher who said, "Fiction is like a dream" and urged us to use "the closely observed detail" in our descriptions.

Writing the Breakout Novel
Donald Maas (Writer's Digest Books 2001)

Especially relevant to suspense writers, this book advises the would-be breakout author to Think Big—to create characters larger than life who face huge challenges with a lot at stake. Sounds obvious, until you sit in front of your computer and try it. Since Maas is a literary agent who represents, among others, Anne Perry, he understands the mystery–suspense field and has the success to back up his assertions.

Story
Robert McKee (HarperCollins 1997)

McKee has guru status in Hollywood as a longtime teacher of screenwriting. His course costs $300 for a weekend of intensive lectures, which makes the hefty price for this hefty hardcover a bargain by comparison. His insights on scene structure and the gap between expectation and reality are alone worth the cost of the book. (If after reading this book, you understand The Negation of the Negation, please e-mail me and explain it!)

The Weekend Novelist Writes a Mystery
Robert Ray (Dell 1998)

Ray also covers crafting the scene at length, and it is to him that I owe the concept of storyboarding the scene before committing actual prose. He infuses this exceptional how-to book with a spiritual quality seldom encountered in books on mystery writing, and his insights into the form are worth reading even if you're not a writer.

Writing the Thriller
T. Macdonald Skillman (Writer's Digest Books 2000)

This book concentrates on the suspense side of the equation and has a useful breakdown of subgenres. The first half talks about the nuts and bolts of thriller writing, while the second half consists of essays on craft by highly successful practitioners of the art.

The Writer's Journey, 2nd Edition
Christopher Vogler (Michael Wiese Productions 1998)

The Hero's Journey is the focus of this book, which breaks down Joseph Campbell's theory into a framework for screenwriters and novelists. Although Vogler works hard to include female Heroes, the Campbell material itself comes with an intrinsic masculine orientation that is difficult to ignore if you're writing feminist mysteries. Still, it's vital to understand the Journey if only because editors now expect certain kinds of books to follow the template.

II. Theoretical Underpinnings

Not everybody likes taking things apart. Some readers and writers prefer to leave their favorite books intact and have no desire to see the pulleys and levers at work. These writers will see no benefit to scholarly studies of the mystery genre, and may even feel that such study can only produce stilted, academic, dry and dull books.

I disagree. I like theory, I feel a need to understand why things are as they are, and I enjoy looking at things I take for granted through new perspectives. So theory has been an important part of my development as a writer, and I encourage those with a bent toward understanding the history and philosophy of mystery fiction to follow me into the halls of academia.

The trouble is that many of these books are marginally available at best. Some are out of print altogether, some verge on the out of print, and others are hard to find. Mystery bookstores with large "used" sections, Amazon.com, and Powell's Books Online are good places to start if you'd like to add scholarly examinations of crime writing to your writer's bookshelf.

Detective Fiction: Crime and Compromise
Dick Allen and David Chacko (Harcourt, Brace, Jovanovich 1974)

Essentially a text for a literature course in mystery fiction, this book contains excerpts of short stories and novels by authors from Poe to Ross Macdonald as well as several essays about the form, including W.H. Auden's "The Guilty Vicarage" and Raymond Chandler's "The Simple Art of Murder."

A Talent to Deceive: An Appreciation of Agatha Christie
Robert Barnard (Mysterious Press 1987)

Barnard brings his wonderfully dry style to this discussion of the Queen of Crime. He makes the case that her genius lay in the way she continually played with the reader's expectations in such a way as to lull even the most astute of readers into missing the clues she planted, in true play-fair fashion, in plain view.

The Reader and the Detective Story
George Dove (Bowling Green State University Popular Press 1997)

You don't actually have to know the meaning of "hermeneutics" to get something out of this book, but it would help. We're in high scholarship here, but an old-time mystery reader like me can enjoy being the subject of semiotic analysis. What is it that we addictive readers bring to the mystery that makes it essentially an interactive experience? Short answer: we understand that we're playing a game and we're reading with one eye on what conventional rabbit the author's going to pull out of his hat this time, comparing it to what someone else did with similar material in a prior book. We *want* the writer to give us the mixture as before, with just enough twist to keep us off-balance. If knowing why things work is important to you, then this book will be, too.

The Art of the Mystery Story
Howard Haycraft

This huge compilation of essays has two drawbacks: it's out of print, and it was published in the 1940s. With those caveats, it's still worthwhile owning, since the essays are seminal in the development of mystery theory.

Delightful Murder: A Social History of the Crime Story
Ernest Mandel (University of Minnesota Press 1985)

Mandel begins with Poe, outlining the ways in which he established the template for the tale of detection, then follows the history of the genre through the country-house period, the emergence of the Hard-boiled Dick, and modern variations on the old styles. One of his theses: the mystery novel observes and reflects the society in which it is written better than any other form of fiction.

Mortal Consequences: From Detective Story to Crime Novel
Julian Symons (Mysterious Press 1993)

As much history as critique, this book gives the reader a broad overview of developments in the mystery on both sides of the Atlantic to about 1970. For the writer, most useful as a means of realizing the depth of what has gone before, and the near-impossibility of coming up with a plot, clue, or gimmick that hasn't been done.

III. Fiction To Learn From _____

These are the books I mentioned in the course of this book as examples of various points I wanted to make. The best part of reading them is that they entertain as they teach. The worst part is that some are out of print—but then that's a good excuse for a trip to a used bookstore, and what could be better than that? Enjoy:

Affair of the Bloodstained Egg Cosy, James Anderson
Aunt Dimity's Death, Nancy Atherton
Fête Fatale, Robert Barnard
Snapshot, Linda Barnes
Blind Descent, Nevada Barr
Eight Million Ways to Die, The Burglar Who Traded Ted Williams,
    Lawrence Block

The Neon Rain, Purple Cane Road, James Lee Burke
Dear Irene, Hocus, Jan Burke
The Hunt for Red October, Tom Clancy
A Stranger Is Watching, A Cry in the Night, Mary Higgins Clark
City of Bones, The Poet, Void Moon, Michael Connelly
Coma, Robin Cook
Hostage, Robert Crais
Jurassic Park, Airframe, Michael Crichton
Catering to Nobody, Diane Mott Davidson
A Maiden's Grave, Jeffery Deaver
Rebecca, Daphne du Maurier
Rogue Wave, Time Expired, Susan Dunlap
Killer on the Road, James Ellroy
Nerve, Whip Hand, Odds Against, Reflex, Dick Francis
A Traitor to Memory, Deception on His Mind, Elizabeth George
Life Support, Tess Gerritsen
A Is for Alibi, J Is for Judgment, Sue Grafton
The Firm, John Grisham
Red Dragon, Silence of the Lambs, Thomas Harris
The Christie Caper, Carolyn G. Hart
Ruling Passions, Pictures of Perfection, Bones and Silence, Reginald Hill
The Night Manager, The Spy Who Came in from the Cold, John Le Carré
The Bootlegger's Daughter, Home Fires, Southern Discomfort, Margaret
    Maron
If Ever I Return, Pretty Peggy-O, Sharyn McCrumb
The Tragedy of Y, Ellery Queen
Little Saigon, T. Jefferson Parker
No Safe Place, Protect and Serve, Richard North Patterson
Dead Crazy, Generous Death, I.O.U., Nancy Pickard
Harry Potter and the Sorcerer's Stone, J.K. Rowling
China Trade, Concourse, S.J. Rozan
Anatomy of a Murder, Robert Traver
Presumed Innocent, Scott Turow
The Red Scream, Under the Beetle's Cellar, All the Dead Lie Down, Mary
    Willis Walker
So Shall You Reap, Marilyn Wallace
The Ice House, Minette Walters
The Ax, Donald Westlake
Fresh Kills, Carolyn Wheat

Index

Lynn Ford

About the Author

Carolyn Wheat, a former defense attorney, is an inspirational writing teacher and award-winning mystery writer. Two of her six Cass Jameson novels were nominated for Edgar awards, and she has won the Anthony, Agatha, Macavity, and Shamus awards for her short stories. She currently teaches at the University of California, San Diego, while also leading mystery tours of the West Coast and working on her next book. She may be e-mailed at cgwheat@pacbell.net.

MORE MYSTERIES
🙂 FROM PERSEVERANCE PRESS 🙂
For the New Golden Age

Available now—

Death, Bones, and Stately Homes, A Tori Miracle Pennsylvania Dutch Mystery
by Valerie S. Malmont
ISBN 1-880284-65-0
Finding a tuxedo-clad skeleton, Tori Miracle fears it could halt Lickin Creek's annual
house tour. While dealing with disappearing and reappearing bodies, a stalker, and an escaped convict, Tori unravels the secrets of the Bride's House and Morgan Manor, which
the townsfolk wish to hide.

Slippery Slopes and Other Deadly Things, A Carrie Carlin Biofeedback Mystery
by Nancy Tesler
ISBN 1-880284-64-2
Biofeedback practitioner/single mom/amateur sleuth Carrie Carlin is up to her neck in
snow, sex, and strangulation when her stress management convention is interrupted by
murder on the slopes of a Vermont ski resort.

Another Fine Mess, **A Bridget Montrose Mystery**
by Lora Roberts
ISBN 1-880284-54-5
Bridget Montrose wrote a surprise bestseller, but now her publisher wants another one. A
writers' retreat seems the perfect opportunity to work in the rarefied company of other
authors…except that one of them has a different ending in mind.

Flash Point, **A Susan Kim Delancey Mystery**
by Nancy Baker Jacobs
ISBN 1-880284-56-1
A serial arsonist is killing young mothers in the Bay Area. Now Susan Kim Delancey,
California's newly appointed chief arson investigator, is in a race against time to catch the
murderer and find the dead women's missing babies—before more lives end in flames.

Open Season on Lawyers, **A Novel of Suspense**
by Taffy Cannon
ISBN 1-880284-51-0
Somebody is killing the sleazy attorneys of Los Angeles. LAPD Detective Joanna Davis
matches wits with a killer who tailors each murder to a specific abuse of legal practice.
They call him The Atterminator—and he likes it.

Too Dead To Swing, **A Katy Green Mystery**
by Hal Glatzer
ISBN 1-880284-53-7
It's 1940, and musician Katy Green joins an all-female swing band touring California by
train—but she soon discovers that somebody's out for blood. First book publication of the
award-winning audio-play. Cast of characters, illustrations, and map included.

The Tumbleweed Murders, A Claire Sharples Botanical Mystery
by Rebecca Rothenberg, completed by Taffy Cannon
ISBN 1-880284-43-X
Microbiologist Sharples explores the musical, geological, and agricultural history of California's Central Valley, as she links a mysterious disappearance a generation earlier to a newly discovered skeleton and a recent death.

Keepers, A Port Silva Mystery
by Janet LaPierre
Shamus Award nominee, *Best Paperback Original 2001*
ISBN 1-880284-44-8
Patience and Verity Mackellar, a Port Silva mother-and-daughter private investigative team, unravel a baffling missing-persons case and find a reclusive religious community hidden on northern California's Lost Coast.

Blind Side, A Connor Westphal Mystery
by Penny Warner
ISBN 1-880284-42-1

The Kidnapping of Rosie Dawn, A Joe Barley Mystery
by Eric Wright
Barry Award, *Best Paperback Original 2000*. Edgar, Ellis, and Anthony Award nominee
ISBN 1-880284-40-5

Guns and Roses, An Irish Eyes Travel Mystery
by Taffy Cannon
Agatha and Macavity Award nominee, *Best Novel 2000*
ISBN 1-880284-34-0

Royal Flush, A Jake Samson & Rosie Vicente Mystery
by Shelley Singer
ISBN 1-880284-33-2

Baby Mine, A Port Silva Mystery
by Janet LaPierre
ISBN 1-880284-32-4

Forthcoming—

Silence Is Golden, A Connor Westphal Mystery
by Penny Warner
Amidst the biggest gold rush since Sutter yelled, "Eureka!" Connor copes with stray gold nuggets, gold teeth, old mining claims, a body in a mineshaft, and the cochlear implant controversy.

The Beastly Bloodline, A Delilah Doolittle Pet Detective Mystery
by Patricia Guiver
Wild horses ordinarily couldn't drag Delilah to a dude ranch. But when a wealthy client asks her to solve the mysterious death of a valuable show horse, she runs into some rude dudes trying to cut her out of the herd—and finds herself on a trail ride to murder.